To: Mimi

From: Little Weasel

Christmas – 1954

Please return me when your
through. cause books get awful
homesick too. tll.

The Black Cat's Clue

MY BOOK

Melissa Rick

The Famous JUDY BOLTON *Mystery Stories*

By MARGARET SUTTON

In Order of Publication

"Judy!" Holly screamed. "I do see a transparent form!"

A Judy Bolton Mystery

THE BLACK CAT'S CLUE

BY

Margaret Sutton

Grosset & Dunlap

PUBLISHERS   NEW YORK

Contents

Contents

The Black Cat's Clue

CHAPTER I

Haunted Houses

"My dear brother," said Judy, looking at Horace in that patient way that used to infuriate him so when they were children, "you know as well as I do that it's perfectly ridiculous to try and get a haunted-house story for a Sunday feature. Who's going to haunt your house?"

"A ghost, of course."

Horace's voice was quiet. But there was a twinkle in his eyes.

Judy sighed deeply.

"After all the mysteries we've solved, it does seem as though you'd outgrow that idea. You thought we were going to have a swell haunted-house story when we first moved to Farringdon, but what happened? No ghost!"

"No, but there were some pretty weird goings on in the house before we moved into it."

"I know," Judy admitted. "And afterwards," she added. "It was exciting, wasn't it? Too exciting! That house still creaks and rattles. I'm glad I don't have to live in it any more. Remember the attic, and that room upstairs where we heard the chimes? And when we kept hearing the whistling in the cellar, you were sure—"

Here Horace interrupted.

"No, my dear sister, *you* were sure it was a ghost. I was merely the innocent victim of your suspicions."

"You don't need to look so innocent now. Where is this 'haunted house' that is going to provide you with your thrilling headlines?" Judy asked.

Horace stood up. The chair in which he had been sitting continued to rock gently, and the old-fashioned clock on the mantel ticked quietly, as its pendulum swung back and forth—back and forth—behind the little decorated glass door.

The clock had belonged to Judy's grandmother, who had left her the house in Dry Brook Hollow, just outside of Roulsville. It was now transformed into what Judy and Peter liked to call their dream house. But, at times, it seemed every bit as spooky as the so-called haunted house in Farringdon.

"Well, aren't you going to answer my question?" Judy asked teasingly, when her brother remained silent.

"Me-aurr!" came from the doorway to the kitchen.

Blackberry stood there rubbing against the door frame and purring so loudly that he could be heard all the way into the living room.

"Don't you *ever* feed your cat, sis?" asked Horace, shaking his head at Judy reproachfully.

"Of course I do," Judy retorted. "He doesn't look starved, does he? Is it my fault if he turns up his nose at the food I give him? Maybe he'd rather catch his dinner in the woods. Anyway, you don't have to tease me about it, Horace Bolton. You haven't grown up a bit."

At this point Peter walked in from the room that had once been Grandma Smeed's parlor bedroom. Now it was the office of the resident FBI agent for three counties in northern Pennsylvania, including the county in which both Farringdon and Roulsville were situated. Peter Dobbs was that resident agent, and Judy was his secretary as well as his wife.

"No," Peter said now, grinning. "Horace hasn't grown up a bit, and neither have you. You still argue like a couple of children."

"But Horace insists there's a haunted house around here that's going to give him copy for a thrilling newspaper story, and he won't tell me where it is," Judy protested.

"Might as well tell her, Horace," Peter said. "She'll find out somehow. Leave it to Judy!"

"I think I'll do just that," said Horace calmly. "But

before I go, I'll give her a hint. Do you remember, Judy, when you were in grade school Longfellow used to be your favorite poet?"

"Which Longfellow?" asked Judy, pretending not to know what Horace was talking about. "There were two of them, you know, Samuel and Henry. I believe they were brothers."

"I'm talking about Henry. They don't teach Samuel in grade school. You're just trying to confuse me."

"Me? Trying to confuse *you?* Oh, Horace!"

"I shall ignore that remark," Horace stated blandly. "As I was saying," he continued, "you used to like Longfellow. He used to be your favorite poet. Isn't that true?"

"I still like him," Judy admitted. "In fact, I've been rereading his poetry since we returned from our vacation. Horace, did you know that his *Song of Hiawatha* was based on some of the Indian legends Peter and I heard while we were up there on the Ojibwa reservation?"

"You mean on Fog Island? If you call that experience a vacation—"

"Well, it was, once we got things straightened out," Judy insisted. "That's why I'm rereading *Hiawatha*, not just the part we studied in school, but the whole thing. Longfellow must have foreseen what was going to happen to all those beautiful old Indian legends if someone didn't do something to preserve them. I always liked his shorter poems, too. 'The Builders,' for instance—"

"But did you ever hear this one?" asked Horace. "It's called 'Haunted Houses,' and it begins:

" *'All houses wherein men have lived and died*
 Are haunted houses. Through the open doors
 The harmless phantoms on their errands glide,
 With feet that make no sound upon the floors.

" *'We meet them at the doorway, on the stair—'* "

"Cut it out, Horace," Peter interrupted. "That's enough of that creepy stuff."

Judy looked at him in surprise.

"Oh, but I was enjoying it," she protested. "I'd like to hear the rest."

"I haven't memorized the whole thing. Anyway," Horace confessed, "I was only teasing. I miss having a little sister around the house to tease. You would have to get married ahead of me. I guess Grandma knew what was cooking, all right, when she willed her house to you. Though I can't help wondering what she'd think if she could come back in spirit and see what you've done to the place."

"Why?" demanded Judy. "Don't you think she'd like it?"

"Like what? The house or the garden?" asked Horace. "She'd hardly recognize either one. Oh, I know it's more romantic the way you and Peter have fixed it up. Most people would like it better, but not Grandma—"

"And are you in a position to know exactly what your grandmother would like?" asked Peter innocently.

Horace grinned.

"You know me. 'The spirit world around this world of sense—' "

"If you're quoting from that spooky poem again, you can just stop it," Judy interrupted. "Peter doesn't like it, and now I'm not so sure I do either."

"Ha! So it's a conspiracy against me. I suppose married people do have to stick together. Me, I've got spurs that jingle, jangle, jingle—"

"I know, and they say, 'Aren't you glad you're single?' I remember that song, too. Never mind, someday someone's going to learn to love you. And you aren't such a bad brother even if you do pick on me. But let's not do it any more. Just to show you you're forgiven," Judy finished, "I'll invite you to lunch. There's pie for dessert."

Horace's grin spread all over his face, and Peter beamed at Judy. He was as proud of her cooking as he was of everything else she did.

"I was hoping there would be," Peter said. "There's nobody who can make pie like my Judy."

"In that case, I'll stay," Horace accepted grandly.

No more was said about haunted houses during lunch. Instead, Judy and Peter talked of the Indians they had met on Big Face Reservation earlier in the summer. They talked of the mystery of the Spirit of Fog Island, of the Indian legends they had heard, of the primitive music.

"I don't think I'll ever hear music again without feeling a little of what the Indians call 'spirit power,'" confessed Judy.

"Music," Horace repeated. For a moment he seemed to be listening to something.

Judy and Peter looked at each other. Then Peter asked, "Is the radio on?"

"I don't think so."

Judy rose and walked across the kitchen to the shelf over the sink, where she kept her little radio. She liked to listen to it while she was washing dishes.

"It's turned off," she said, mystified. "Why? Did you hear anything?"

"No, but Horace seemed to be listening," Peter began.

"Can't a man listen to silence?" asked Horace in pretended surprise.

"What man?" asked Judy, making a face at him. "Shall I cut you a man-sized piece of pie, or would you prefer the usual?"

"Better take the usual," Peter advised. "Then you'll get a second helping. It's apple. Smell the cinnamon."

Horace did full justice to his first piece.

"You know, sis," he declared as he passed his plate for a second helping, "if I ever find a girl who can make pies like this, I think I'll take the fatal leap. Honey could draw a picture on the top, but her crust is like biting into a piece of cardboard."

"Hardly that bad," Peter defended her.

Honey was Peter's sister. The firm where she worked was expanding. Now, instead of simply designing patterns, the Dean Individual Stamp Company designed dress materials. Honey was their only artist, but Mr. Dean was planning to hire more girls if he could find them. His son, Forrest Dean, was Horace's chief rival for Honey's affections and was, Judy felt, the reason for her brother's sour-grapes attitude in regard to Honey's artistic ability.

"She works too hard over her pies," Judy said. "The secret is to toss the shortening in lightly. I'll have to show her."

"Why don't you ask her over for tonight?" Peter suggested.

"Why tonight?" asked Horace. "Is it some special occasion? If so, I think I'll stick around."

"It's *Honey's* company I want," declared Judy. "She doesn't quote spooky poetry and listen to sounds that aren't there. Peter has to leave right after lunch on one of his mysterious assignments. He may be gone for days, and this house is—well, it is going to be sort of lonesome without him."

Horace turned to Peter apologetically.

"Golly!" he said. "Why doesn't someone tell me these things? I didn't mean—"

"Forget it," said Peter. "A mere haunted house, wherever it is, can't frighten Judy. Am I right, Angel?"

Judy kissed him for an answer. Then she handed him his portfolio. Peter was ready to leave. Horace offered to drive him to the station in his new coffee-colored convertible.

"I think, this time, I'll say good-bye at the house. I don't like coming back to it—empty," Judy explained.

Peter gave her a worried glance and she added quickly, "I don't mind being alone when I'm busy, though. I'll have that report in the mail by tomorrow. You'll see."

There was still a long report for Judy to type on the mystery that had made her visit to the Indian reservation such an unforgettable experience. The report was important. After what had happened on Fog Island Peter had been kept busy all summer straightening out things with the Bureau of Indian Affairs. The trip to Fog Island had been followed by a busy week in Washington where Judy had toured FBI headquarters with Peter. She had no idea what his latest assignment was, but she did know what needed to be done to wind up the mystery they had solved for the Indians.

"I'll be back as soon as I can, Angel," Peter said as

he kissed her good-bye. "On my next trip I'll try to take you with me. You know I'd take you along this time if I could. Just call the field office if you should need me."

"Take it easy, sis, and forget that poem I quoted," Horace added. "I'm afraid I didn't pick a very appropriate time."

Judy laughed, but when the car had gone she still stood with her hand on the doorknob.

"I should say you didn't, Horace," she answered him in her thoughts. "*All houses wherein men have lived and died are haunted* . . . And both Grandma and Grandpa died in this very house less than two years ago."

CHAPTER II

"No Sound upon the Floors"

"THAT brother of mine!" Judy said to herself as she opened the door. "I hope he didn't mean *this* house!"

Inside, everything was quiet—too quiet.

As Judy moved about the table, clearing away the dishes and putting the food away, she tried to tell herself it wasn't the same house it had been when her grandparents lived in it. Certainly it didn't look the same. It had been redecorated from top to bottom, a new picture window put in where the old "everyday door" used to be, and all the old-fashioned "gingerbread" ripped out. The huge stone fireplaces in both the living room and kitchen Judy loved. She also loved the big rooms with their low, beamed ceilings and wide floorboards . . . *"With feet that make no sound"* . . .

Determined to put the bothersome lines Horace had quoted out of her mind, Judy marched into Peter's den, pulled the typewriter table out into the bay window where the light was best, and began to type as fast as accuracy allowed.

With her papers on the window seat to the right of her, Judy could look out on the garden as she typed. Light from the window behind her made her notes easy to read. But after a while she found herself unable to concentrate on her work.

The garden made her think of another mystery that she half wished she had left unsolved. Even the flowers seemed to miss the little girl who had planted them.

"I wish Roberta were here," thought Judy.

But here she broke off to scold herself again. She had known her little boarder couldn't stay here forever, and she was happier with her own people. Just the same, Judy couldn't forget that now, whenever Peter's business took him away overnight, she had to stay all alone in the house.

It was lovely in the garden at this time of the day. A light breeze played among the tall spears of phlox and delphinium. Nothing else moved except one white butterfly fluttering above the flowers. Judy, still trying to concentrate on Indians, remembered their belief in the butterfly as a spirit.

Me-mem-gme, they had called it. Judy was recalling more of her adventures on Fog Island, and adding them to her notes, when she glanced up and saw, through the window, a transparent form in purple . . .

"Oh, no!" she cried aloud and started up from her chair, almost tipping it over in her excitement. She couldn't have seen what she thought she saw! Some trick of light had made her imagine she saw her grandmother walking in the garden. Or was it a subconscious fear Horace had put in her mind?

Her heart still thumping inside her, Judy hurried out to investigate. Something more definite than either fear or imagination must have caused the apparition. But what?

Outside, there was nothing to explain it—nothing at all. The garden was deserted. There was no sign of anyone having been there. And yet someone must have been!

"That *was* my grandmother's purple dress," thought Judy uneasily.

Through the trees that grew along the edge of Dry Brook, she could just see the cars on the main road between Farringdon and Roulsville. But none of them had stopped or turned down the little road that crossed the brook and ended at the house that now seemed so unutterably lonely.

On either side of the house, beyond the immediate grounds, were the pastures of adjoining farms—Bundy's on the left and Potter's on the right. A few cows were to be seen grazing on the hillside, among them Judy's own Daisy. It was too early for Red Burnett, who worked the farm on shares, to be coming to milk Daisy. Anyway, the transparent form Judy had seen was that of a woman—an elderly woman in purple, who seemed to flit, like the white butterfly, just a little above the ground.

Judy listened. She could hear no sound except the soft talking noises of her chickens as they walked about in their wire enclosure beyond the garden. A bird trilled a little song, then flew away. Judy could just hear a car passing on the distant main road. But that was all. None of these sounds explained anything.

Behind the house was a wooded hill. As Judy turned to look once more in that direction, the sun went under a cloud. Could the sun have caused some kind of weird reflection? If so, Judy couldn't figure out how.

For half an hour she searched the garden in vain. Then she sat down on one of the two stone benches beside the path and fell into contemplation. But the mystery of death was something she knew she could not solve any more than she could solve the mystery of life.

The sky had clouded over while Judy looked for the least sign of anyone having been in the garden. Now it started to rain, and she had to go inside. She shivered as something that she could neither see nor hear seemed to walk in beside her.

"It was a gust of wind, nothing more," Judy told herself irritably.

She went straight to the telephone and called Honey.

"Yes?" said a quavering voice at the other end of the wire.

It was Peter's grandmother, who was still living, although she was very old and almost helpless. Judy asked after her health and heard a long account of both Grandma's and Grandpa's ailments before she ventured the question: "Is Honey there?"

"She isn't coming home for dinner tonight," Grandma Dobbs told her. "That nice young Mr. Dean asked her to help him celebrate his birthday. Wasn't that thoughtful of him?"

Horace wouldn't think so. But it served him right. Him and his haunted houses! The old meanie, criticizing Honey's attempts at pie-making! Judy remembered some of her own cakes. They hadn't bothered Peter. He had ignored the failures and praised the successes. Judy was still far from being a perfect cook, but she did make good pies. And it would have been fun to show Honey her secret.

Murmuring something polite, Judy said good-bye to Grandma Dobbs and abandoned the idea of telephoning any of her other friends, now that she knew Honey probably would be out late and couldn't stay all night with her. Lois would be out with Donald

Carter, anyway, and Lorraine, who had been married the same day as Judy, would not want to leave Arthur to spend the evening by himself.

"Anyway," said Judy, picking up her cat and cuddling him, "I have you, Blackberry. Or would you rather prowl through the woods than stay with me?"

The cat's answer was a contented purr. Judy turned on some music and sat quietly petting her cat and listening for almost half an hour. Then Blackberry leaped from her lap and went to the door.

"I knew it wouldn't last," Judy sighed as she let him out.

The music had stopped. Now, a frenzied voice was telling Judy about a new home permanent that would make her as glamorous as a movie star. Quite satisfied with her own naturally wavy auburn hair, she tried to relax and listen to the news that followed.

"If only they'd tell us about some of the good things that happened in the world!" she thought as she listened. "But the news is always about some disaster."

The rain that had driven her indoors might be the tail end of the hurricane that had swept through Florida the week before, taking many lives. A train had been derailed, and property damage was estimated far into the millions.

News of a bank robbery followed. That could be the reason for Peter's sudden summons.

"He'd keep me out of that, I know," thought Judy.

"He always tries to keep me out of anything connected with desperate criminals."

Judy was worried about Peter. What was he investigating? He couldn't tell her. She knew that. None of her questions seemed to have any answers.

Finally, after fixing herself a sandwich and pouring out a glass of milk that she couldn't finish, Judy went back to her typing and completed her report of a mystery that she had been able to solve. Seldom had a single evening dragged on so long.

And all the time Judy felt the invisible presence of the transparent figure she had glimpsed that afternoon when the sun was shining. She laughed a little to herself. Had it come in with her, and was it even now flitting about the house, perhaps disapproving of the changes she had made?

"*We meet them at the doorway, on the stair . . .*" Judy repeated to herself when, at last, she started upstairs to bed.

She couldn't help wondering what the rest of the poem was. Now she half wished Peter had let Horace finish it. Maybe it would explain the phantom she had seen in the garden.

Judy had a book of favorite poems by Henry Wadsworth Longfellow, but apparently "Haunted Houses" was not one of the favorites chosen.

Still puzzled about the poem, Judy finally fell asleep.

In the morning, awakened by the bright sunlight that poured in the windows, she laughed at her nervousness of the night before.

"Maybe I like to be alone. Maybe I like to scare myself with apparitions and spooky poetry," she said to herself as she chose a bright plaid blouse and green skirt to match. Tying a green band around her hair to keep it from blowing in the wind, she was ready. But for what?

Through the bay window the garden was beautiful in the morning sunshine. No transparent figure was walking there now. Phlox, zinnias, marigolds and dahlias were all in bloom, and everything looked so bright and fresh after the rain that Judy could hardly wait to get outside.

"I'll take the car and go somewhere this morning," she decided. "What I need is to talk with someone more companionable than a ghost."

CHAPTER III

Sad News

Just as Judy was backing the car out of the garage, Red Burnett hailed her. He was coming to milk Daisy, and had brought the morning paper as he always did. Judy took it, thanked him, and was about to drive on when he said, "We've lost a good neighbor."

"We have?" asked Judy in surprise. "I know we're getting a lot of new ones with all the building going on below, but they aren't too close. I didn't know we'd lost any—"

"Well, we have," Red interrupted gravely. "I guess you didn't see the complete list of dead in that train wreck after the Florida hurricane."

"I saw it in yesterday's paper, but I didn't read it very carefully," Judy admitted. "I don't know anybody in Florida. Or do I?"

Red had given her such an odd look that the question came as an afterthought.

"I'm afraid you do. David Potter's name was on the list," he said.

"David Potter!" Judy exclaimed. "Oh, Red! I didn't know he was in Florida. Why, he's our nearest neighbor and a dear old man if ever there was one. He was wonderful to my grandparents, and I remember, even as a little girl, how much I liked to hear him sing. He and Sam Tucker and Waldo Abson used to get together and sing the most beautiful ballads. It seems to me someone told me David Potter composed them himself."

"I heard that he did, too. There was one song about wanting too much that just about fits these times," Red said.

Judy hadn't heard that one.

"The one I remember best was called 'The Man Who Works His Way,' * and I'm sure it must have been his own composition, because we had to have his permission, Grandpa said, before we could revise it for a school song. It began:

> " *'The world is wide; the sky is blue;*
> *The future fair is waiting you . . .'* "

Red grinned at Judy's attempt to recall the original ballad.

"It beats all what comes into a person's mind,

* By Victor L. Beebe

doesn't it?" he asked. "I was just thinking—old David Potter may be dead, but that music of his—"

"You're right," Judy agreed. "None of us will ever forget his music. Grandma was especially fond of it. She used to tell him he ought to get it published, but I guess he couldn't be bothered. He didn't like crowds and never went anywhere if he could help it. That's why I can't understand his being in Florida. You're sure it wasn't some other David Potter who was killed in the hurricane?"

Red shook his head.

"No, it was our neighbor, all right. I knew he'd gone to Florida. He was getting up some kind of a family reunion and expected to bring his son home with him."

"His son! I didn't even know he had one," Judy exclaimed.

"I guess there's plenty about old David Potter that none of us knew," declared Red as he started on toward the barn.

"Red!"

He didn't hear her. It was probably just as well. Judy started the car, but she couldn't help thinking, "Grandma knew. I'm sure she did. Grandma knew so much that she never told anybody. I wonder . . ."

But Judy dismissed the thought. It was perfectly ridiculous to suppose her grandmother had come back in spirit to tell her any of the secrets she had kept during her lifetime. There must be some logical explanation for the purple apparition, and Judy was determined to find out what it was.

At the main road she stopped the car and looked in both directions before she turned toward Roulsville. She had thought of taking the longer road to Farringdon and spending the day with her parents. She couldn't tell her mother what she had seen without worrying her. But she could certainly tell that exasperating brother of hers.

"Maybe I'll drive to Farringdon and have a talk with him later," she decided. "And I'll find out the rest of that poem if it's the last thing I do."

First she would mail her report to Peter and have a quiet breakfast in Roulsville.

"Someone I know may be eating at Joe's place," she thought as she parked the car and went into the diner.

Most of the counter stools were occupied by men. Only one other girl was having breakfast there, and at first Judy couldn't recall ever having seen her before.

Apparently, the girl was a few years younger than Judy. She seemed so plain and awkward and frightened that Judy, who had taken the seat next to her, longed to say something that would make her feel more at ease. But what could she say?

She might have thought of something if Joe hadn't come to take her order just then.

"How's the famous girl detective?" he asked. "I saw

in the papers how you found that little girl's folks for her. I kind of miss her, though. Such a bright little face!"

"I miss her too," said Judy.

She didn't feel like thinking about Roberta and how very much she missed her, or about the garden they had planted together—the garden where she had seen —but just what had she seen? That flash of purple was nothing. Judy had almost convinced herself that she had only imagined it, when the girl on the stool beside her spoke.

"Pardon me," she said, and her voice trembled a little, "did I hear the waiter call you a detective?"

"He was only joking," Judy replied. "Of course," she added modestly, "I have solved a few mysteries."

"You're not, by any chance, the Judy Bolton whose grandparents used to live in Dry Brook Hollow? But you are!" she exclaimed, looking at Judy more closely. "Oh, maybe you can help me!"

"I can try," said Judy. "Anyway, I can listen while you tell me about yourself. I feel I ought to know you, too, but I don't quite place you. Let's carry our breakfasts over to one of the booths. We can talk more privately there. Those little pitchers up there on the shelf behind the counter may have big ears."

The girl laughed.

Now, Judy wondered why on earth she had thought her plain at first. Her mouth was too wide and her hair too drab a brown for real beauty. But she was lovely when she laughed, because she laughed with her eyes, too. They were a strange shade of blue. Everything about the girl was suddenly strange and exciting.

"From here on," Judy told herself resolutely, "I'll forget my own foolish fancies and concentrate on whatever is bothering her."

CHAPTER IV

The Girl Without a Birthday

"MY NAME's Holly," the girl began when they had found a booth and carried over their cups and plates, "and since we're going to be confidential I may as well tell you the whole story. My mother named me Holly because I was born on Christmas."

"How nice!" Judy began.

"You may think so, but it isn't, really. It just means I haven't any birthday. Oh, people send me presents at Christmas, of course, and sometimes they remember to say 'Happy Birthday' too. But it's always just one present and hardly ever anything I really want."

"What do you really want?" asked Judy.

The girl pondered this for a moment. Then her strange blue eyes grew dreamy.

25

"I want so much—so very much! I want to be rich and famous some day. I want people to respect me and maybe love me a little. And I want a home. I mean a real home with a mother and father. But that's impossible. My parents are both dead. Cousin Cleo brought me up. She's here. They're all here. It's sort of a family reunion. All the relatives are flocking around Uncle David like flies around sugar, now that he's rich. It's disgusting. I wasn't going to come, but then I got to thinking how there ought to be at least one person at the reunion who really loved him. So I just came without letting anyone know. Do you think it will be all right?"

The question was so unexpected that Judy gave a little gasp, without meaning to.

"You came to visit your uncle?" she asked, suddenly apprehensive. "You say his name is David—"

"Yes, David Potter. He's my favorite uncle, in fact, the only one of my relatives I knew before Mother died. She was little and frail, with red-gold hair—like yours only maybe a little lighter. My sister Doris looks like her, but I'm all Potter, Dad used to say. Dad wasn't frail, at least not until after Mother died. Then his health went, too. I was only six when we used to come to visit Uncle David. Doris was ten and Ruth twelve. You must remember us a little."

"I do now," Judy said. "I remember meeting Ruth and Doris on that path that goes through the woods to your uncle's farm. Once you tagged along and cried because we wouldn't let you play with us. It was thoughtless—"

"Oh, that's all right," Holly broke in before Judy could finish. "Older sisters never like babies tagging along. They called me Baby, too. Maybe that's why you didn't remember me as Holly. I thought you wouldn't forget Doris and Ruth. And of course you know Uncle David. His house always seemed like a second home to me. He and my father were so much alike. They were both musicians. Oh, I suppose they were farmers, really. But they were musicians at heart. That is what Uncle David likes best about farming, he told me in one of his letters. He said a man could sing while he was working. He didn't need any audience except the birds, he told me. He loves nature and lives simply. But he's always kept the house neat. He knew I'd come back. But what's the matter?" Holly asked.

She had paused in her story long enough to glance at Judy. There were sympathetic tears in Judy's eyes.

"I did know your uncle," Judy said. "I'm so sorry! I hardly know how to tell you, but I'm afraid you've come back too late—"

"Why?" demanded Holly. "He hasn't sold the house, has he? Uncle David wouldn't—"

"No, he hasn't sold it," Judy interrupted gently. "Holly, your uncle David is dead."

"Dead!" exclaimed Holly, a stunned look coming over her face. "But that can't be. Uncle David was strong and healthy. He was never sick—never!"

"It was an accident." Judy spread the paper before her. "He went to Florida to bring his son up here for the reunion, and was killed when the hurricane wrecked the train he was on. Burial was in Florida, it says here—"

"Oh, no! That's too cruel!" exclaimed Holly. "Uncle David will never rest!"

Judy shivered, thinking again of the apparition she had seen in the garden.

"Don't say that!"

"But it's true!" Holly insisted. "Why, he wouldn't even talk of Florida! And that 'devoted' son of his was just as bad as all the rest of the relatives. They never came near him while he was poor. And nobody considered his wishes the least bit. He wanted us to come and live with him after Mother and Daddy died, but the other relatives made such a fuss that finally Uncle David gave up the idea."

"The poor man!" Judy exclaimed. "I wondered why you stopped coming."

"Well, now you know." Holly's voice was bitter. "Oh, they arranged everything. Aunt Flo needed someone to help her with the housework, so she took Ruth. A distant cousin, Arlene Knight, took Doris to Hollywood. She had an idea she could get her in the movies. Nobody really wanted me except Uncle David, but his wife had left him and taken their son with her, and the story had spread around that Uncle David was cruel to them. I never believed it. He was always kind to me. I begged and begged to be allowed to stay with him."

Here Holly paused. She wasn't crying, but her voice had become a little husky. It was a tragic story she was telling. But sometimes it helped to talk about things, Judy knew, and so she listened sympathetically.

"Cousin Cleo was the one who objected the loudest," Holly continued after a moment. "She didn't think it would do unless his wife was there. But that was out. His wife had taken the baby and gone back to her folks in Florida. Uncle David wouldn't even talk about it. So in the end Cousin Cleo had to take me herself. It was her duty! But I was too rebellious, she said, and she had to put me in boarding school.

"Did I say boarding school?" Holly went on. "To me it was more like a prison. Boarding school may be all right for people who make friends easily. But I hated it. I just lived for the time when I'd be old enough to leave that horrible place and come to see Uncle David on my own. And now—he's gone!" she finished with a dry sob. "I just don't see how I can bear it."

"People can bear a lot more than they think they

can," Judy told her soberly. "I know it's hard, but you look like a girl with courage. You'll go on to the next thing and face whatever has to be faced bravely."

"You mean my relatives?"

"It *will* take courage to face them, won't it? I suppose some of them will already be there for the reunion."

Holly sighed deeply.

"Yes, I suppose so."

"I tried to break the news as gently as I could," Judy said, "but it must be an awful shock."

"It is." Holly's lips tightened. "But I might have known something terrible would happen. It always does. Honestly, it's almost as if it had been planned that way. I knew there was something queer about that reunion. Cousin Cleo wrote me at camp that she had received an invitation, but I didn't get any, and neither did Ruth or Doris. They would have written to me about it if they had. They're swell sisters. Ruth is married now. She asked me to come and live with them, but they aren't very well off and have such a tiny apartment that, with a new baby and everything, I knew there wouldn't be room. Doris teaches school and boards around. Aunt Flo disapproves, of course. She disapproves of everything unless it was her idea. I told you how she and Cousin Arlene had it all planned for Doris to be a movie star. Doris is pretty enough. Her hair is just the color of yours, but let anybody call it red—!"

Judy smiled.

"I used to hate being called a redhead, too," she admitted, "but now I don't mind. You see, I married the boy who used to tease me about my hair and he's—wonderful."

"I wish I were old enough to get married," Holly said. "Then I'd have my own home. But I'm only fifteen. Besides, boys are pests."

"They certainly are," agreed Judy, giggling. "I'd be having breakfast at home this morning if my brother—the pest—hadn't quoted some spooky poetry about haunted houses and made me jittery about staying alone. My husband had to leave on a business trip, but he left the car for me. I'll be glad to drive you up to your uncle's house if you want me to."

Holly hesitated.

"I don't know what to do now that he's dead. The house won't be empty, though, with Cousin Cleo and Aunt Florence and all the rest of them there for—for this reunion that you'd think they'd have had the decency to postpone. Oh, it'll be horrible! They'll manage everything! Cousin Cleo is probably 'putting the house to rights,' as she calls it, already. She'll spoil everything I ever cared about!"

"Well, finish your coffee and we'll drive up and see what's happened," urged Judy. "Maybe they didn't come after all and things aren't quite as bad as you think."

CHAPTER V

A Secret Plan

HOLLY finished her coffee quickly. Paying for both breakfasts, Judy picked up the heavy suitcase Holly had brought with her and started for the parking lot where she had left the car.

"That suitcase is too heavy for you," Holly protested, following her. "I've got all my stuff in it. I intended to stay—"

"I see you did. Well, here we are," Judy announced, heaving the suitcase into the luggage compartment of the car. "We'd better keep it here until we know what the score is. It may be just as well if your relatives don't know what your intentions were. I'm not too sure I know them myself," she added as she took her place at the steering wheel. "You told me, but I have to get it straight if I'm going to help you. Did you come because of the reunion?"

"Yes, it looked queer to me," the younger girl declared. "Uncle David hated crowds, and even if he did decide to hold a family reunion, why would he invite the relatives he liked the least and leave out those he cared about?"

"Maybe he didn't. Maybe someone else sent out those invitations," Judy said thoughtfully.

"I'd just like to get hold of one of them," declared Holly. "I'd know Uncle David's handwriting in a minute. He writes to me regularly. I mean, he did. I felt I knew him so well through his letters. They were all that made boarding school bearable. I was always there for the summer camp, too."

"Isn't that any better than school itself?" asked Judy.

"A little," Holly admitted, "but the girls are still watched as if they were prisoners. I wasn't allowed to leave the grounds except with Cousin Cleo. She's my legal guardian. She's probably been notified that I ran away, and won't be very pleased to see me, but I had to come."

"I can see you did. Holly, you said your uncle wrote to you regularly. Do you have any of his letters with you?" Judy asked.

"Yes, in my suitcase. Do you think we could get hold of one of those invitations and compare the handwriting to see if Uncle David wrote them himself?"

"We could try," Judy replied. "There's certainly something odd about all this. But the thing that really puzzles me is why your uncle went to Florida. Couldn't his son have come up here by himself if he wanted to attend the reunion?"

"I should think he could." Holly was puzzled too.

"I didn't even know he had a son until Red told me," Judy continued. "Mr. Potter never spoke of him."

"Who's Red?" asked Holly.

"Red Burnett. He works our farm on shares," Judy explained. "When my grandparents died they left me their farm, and they left Horace the wood lot across the main road, all except the acre of land Red has. Red is a landscape gardener, and he has plenty to do here in Roulsville with all this building going on."

"It looks strange to me around here," said Holly. "I remember it the way it was before the flood."

They had left the business section of Roulsville. Soon they came to the three giant pieces of broken concrete that still stood as a grim reminder of the dam that had broken and flooded the entire town below. Judy stopped the car so that Holly could look out across the valley.

"Luckily, the people were warned in time, and escaped to the hills. But we had to stand there and watch our homes being washed away. Mine was one of them," Judy added.

"Yes, I remember your father was a doctor in Roulsville. Did he go back there after the flood?"

"No," Judy replied. "He set up a new practice in Farringdon. Most of the people whose homes were washed away did go back and rebuild, though. There's a new dam in a safer location below the town. New industries have sprung up, and Roulsville is growing so fast that—well, some people who aren't strictly honest have been making some easy money, as they call it, especially since gas was discovered."

"The gas rush! That's what Cousin Cleo calls it. She told me all about the new gas wells that are being drilled on some of the farms above Roulsville. Yours isn't one of them, is it?"

"No. They're running a pipe line up our way, though, so we'll have gas to use. It's the farmers up the North Hollow road who are lucky—"

"Lucky, did you say? My uncle would have been better off if gas had never been discovered," Holly said. "He was the latest one to strike it rich, I guess. When he was poor the relatives left him alone. They even considered him a little queer, but now he's called a musical genius—or was. I still can't believe he's dead. What will become of all his precious music?"

"We'll see that none of it is destroyed. We really shouldn't have stopped," Judy observed. "See those black clouds gathering overhead? Now I'll have to drive fast to get to your uncle's farm ahead of the rain."

Judy started the car, but before they had gone another mile the storm broke. A great gust of wind swept in from across the valley. The rain descended all at once, beating against the windshield and coming down from the sky as if it were being poured in bucketfuls.

Even with the windshield wiper going, Judy could see but a few feet ahead. She had to drive cautiously to avoid sudden rivers of water that poured across the road from the hill above it.

"It looks as if we're having a private little hurricane of our own," said Holly. "Was it as bad as this just before the flood?"

"Worse," Judy replied, "but this is bad enough."

They had reached the North Hollow road that ended at the Potter farm, but could see nothing but a muddy river pouring into the valley from the cement highway.

Pulling up beside the four mailboxes that marked the road, Judy stopped the car and waited. For half an hour the rain descended in torrents. And when it did finally cease, the North Hollow road was still a sea of mud.

"Can you make it?" Holly asked anxiously.

"The water's draining off. I can try it," Judy said. "Even if we get stuck in the mud, it isn't a very long walk from here."

"I didn't want to arrive looking like a drowned rat.

The relatives consider me the ugly duckling of the family as it is. Oh dear!" Holly said as the car plowed through the mud. "This is awful. I shouldn't have asked you—"

"You didn't," Judy interrupted with a smile. "I offered to drive you over. To tell you the truth, I had the whole day on my hands. I was really looking for something to do with my time."

"You found it all right," Holly said ruefully as the car stalled.

Judy tried to start it, but it refused to budge. The back wheels only spun around in the mud, spattering everything.

"It's no use," she announced. "How do you feel about walking the rest of the way? It isn't far. We've passed the Blade farm. The Millers live in that house just opposite; then the Absons, and after that comes your uncle's place."

"I know. Nothing has changed along this road except—" Holly sighed. "I mean the house won't be the same without Uncle David and his music."

"His own compositions, weren't they?" Judy asked.

"Yes, and old sheet music that's been in the family ever since my great-grandfather's time. The Potters were all musical—all except me. Ruth plays beautifully and Doris sings. I suppose I ought not to tell you this, but I—I try and write the words. I'm better at stories, though. I'm always dreaming up make-believe people. Some day I'm going to put them in a book."

"You are? That's wonderful," declared Judy. "I've always envied people who can write. I wish I could. I've had so many thrilling adventures."

"Like this?" asked Holly. "I suppose you could call it thrilling. Anyway, it's chilling! I really don't mind walking. We'll get our feet wet, though."

"Not if we pull off our shoes and stockings and go barefoot the way we used to. Come on," Judy urged, beginning to remove her own shoes. "We'll leave your heavy suitcase here in the car and if anybody asks—"

"Let me answer the questions," Holly interrupted eagerly. "I have a perfectly swell plan. If it works— but let's try it first. There! I'm ready."

"So am I," agreed Judy.

Carrying their shoes and stockings, the two girls started walking along beside the road where it wasn't so muddy. The short grass felt good under their feet. Presently Holly stopped and picked a daisy.

"They want me. They don't. They want me. They don't," she chanted as she plucked off the petals, one by one.

"Do you mean the relatives?" asked Judy, laughing.

"Yes. They don't. But I don't care."

Holly was laughing, too. The whole thing actually had become an adventure to her. Laughing over every little misfortune along the way, and giggling at the prospect of startling the assembled relatives, she and

Judy continued walking until, at last, they came in sight of the Potter farm.

"It looks deserted, doesn't it?" asked Judy, eyeing the gray structure with suspicion.

Like her own home, it was built partly of native stone and had the appearance of a house that had grown up by itself in its setting of tangled vines and shrubs.

"Deserted, did you say?" Holly asked.

As they approached the house they could hear a woman's strident voice calling from somewhere on the second floor:

"Look in the clock! It's bound to be somewhere."

"Yes, look in the clock!"

"That's Aunt Flo," Holly whispered. "The echo is her daughter, Diana, a 'little girl' of about thirty. She isn't well. Aunt Flo thought she'd *never* raise her. Poor Ruth was supposed to wait on both of them."

"No wonder your sister married young," Judy whispered back. "Who do you suppose is downstairs?"

"Cousin Cleo, no doubt. Now, if my plan works—"

"What is this secret plan of yours?" Judy asked curiously.

"I don't want to tell," Holly said childishly. "You might laugh at me. You'll see soon, though," she promised.

She pulled off a half slip she was wearing, suddenly

deciding she no longer needed it. Tearing it in half, she handed a piece to Judy.

"Here," she said, "let's wipe off the mud and make ourselves presentable. It's dry on the porch. We can put on our shoes and stockings—and look! We can even use the window for a mirror. It's darker inside than it is out here."

A crash as of broken china suddenly made both girls jump. Inside the house someone screamed, "There was a face in that window! I saw it distinctly just now as I came downstairs. Diana and I have had enough of this spooky house—"

"Don't be ridiculous, Flo!" was the sharp rejoinder. "There's someone out there. I saw the face, too, and I have a pretty good idea who it is."

"She saw you, Holly!" Judy whispered.

"Don't I know it!" the younger girl returned with a giggle. "If I'd tried to make a startling appearance I couldn't have done any better. I don't like the sound of things, though. Aunt Flo dropped something when she saw me. I hope it wasn't anything belonging to Uncle David."

"It was china," Judy whispered. "Listen!"

Both girls stood motionless as the harsh voice belonging to Holly's aunt Florence declared, "Well, anyway, it wasn't in the teapot. That's smashed to smithereens. I saved myself the trouble of looking inside—"

"They're searching the house!" exclaimed Holly, forgetting to whisper. "I wonder what they're trying to find."

"We'll soon know," declared Judy as Cousin Cleo stepped out on the porch. She called sharply:

"If that's you out there, Holly Potter, you may as well come in and account for yourself. You and Doris, too."

CHAPTER VI

Playing a Part

"Doris?" Judy whispered.

Holly giggled. "I knew she'd think you were my sister Doris. Are you good at playing a part? If you are, you can really help me—if you will, Judy."

Judy had to decide quickly. "I've done it before," she began.

But before she could quite make up her mind, Cousin Cleo walked around the corner of the porch to where the girls had been only partially concealed, and literally pounced upon them.

"What do you mean by hiding here and listening?" she demanded. "Wasn't it bad enough to help your sister sneak away from camp? Now you have to creep up here like a couple of ghosts and scare the wits out of us."

42

"I—helped Holly sneak away?" Judy questioned, while Holly looked at her imploringly.

"Well, didn't you?" Cleo Potter retorted.

She was obviously a nervous woman who tried to cover up her own nervousness by making other people uncomfortable in her presence.

"Actually, she's scared," thought Judy.

The thought gave her courage. She had no choice now. Whether she wanted to play the part of Doris or not, she found herself playing it.

"Why shouldn't I help Holly?" she asked. "We came for the reunion. We supposed, naturally, that Uncle David would want us. A reunion is supposed to include all the relatives, isn't it?"

"But your uncle David—"

"I know," Judy broke in quickly. "We read about it in the morning paper. It's the first Holly knew of Uncle David's death. It came as an awful shock when she expected to see him alive—"

"And you?"

"I—I was heartbroken," Judy faltered.

The tears that came to her eyes were real and convincing. After a moment she controlled them and said, "I think Uncle David would have wanted you to ask us in. Don't you, Holly?"

"Oh, yes! I most certainly do," the younger girl replied. "He always wanted us—"

"Come in, then! Don't just stand there," another voice said sharply.

This was Holly's aunt Florence who had appeared suddenly, at the door. She was older than Judy had thought she would be from the sound of her voice. In appearance she was a gentle-looking old lady with stooped shoulders and graying hair. The blue print dress she was wearing strengthened this impression. Her voice, however, as she continued scolding Cousin Cleo, was anything but gentle.

"Cleo, you can't turn them out. Where would they stay?" she demanded. "There's a limit, you know. Besides, maybe David did invite them."

"But he didn't. He invited only the six of us. Here it is in his own handwriting."

Cousin Cleo produced a letter which Holly took almost too eagerly.

"Is it his handwriting?" Judy whispered.

"It looks like it, but you can never tell—"

"What are you girls whispering about?" Cousin Cleo interrupted, snatching back the letter.

"We haven't seen each other in a long time. We have a lot to say to each other," Holly said quickly.

"When did you arrive?" Aunt Florence inquired.

Judy answered that one.

"On the morning train. A neighbor drove us up from Roulsville, but the car got stuck in the mud, so we had to leave our things in the car and walk the rest of the way."

"What neighbor?" Cousin Cleo wanted to know.

"Dobbs, I think the name was. I believe they live on the old Smeed farm just over the hill—"

"They do, do they? And I suppose Mr. Dobbs is young and good-looking—"

"Oh, definitely!" Judy said.

"But he's married, worse luck!" Holly added.

With Judy to stand by her, she was really beginning to enjoy herself. Finally the two girls were invited into the living room, which was something like Judy's own except that the absence of a bay window made it a little darker. Instead of windows, two doors, side by side, were in the wall opposite the fireplace. Both were of dark oak, as was the beamed ceiling and all the woodwork in the house. Judy liked it, even if it was dark.

Suddenly one of the doors opened. A tall, gaunt man with thin hair and a sallow complexion stood in the doorway surveying the scene in the living room.

"I thought I heard Holly's voice. Cleo says you weren't invited. What's the idea of coming here to disrupt things?"

"Am I disrupting anything?" Holly asked innocently.

When the man did not answer, Judy whispered to Holly, "Who is he?"

Obviously, it was her move next, but she could think of nothing to say.

"Cousin Fred," Holly whispered back. "He's—"

She didn't finish.

"Is this your sister Doris?" he asked, nodding toward Judy. "I thought she'd show up sooner or later. Hollywood didn't think so much of you, did it, Doris? With that nose— Say, I don't remember Doris as having such a turned-up nose. No wonder the movies didn't want her."

"It was a case of Doris not wanting the movies," Cousin Cleo informed him acidly. "Arlene wrote us all about it, but since you always expect me to answer your personal letters, you wouldn't know about that."

"All right, all right," said Cousin Fred and retreated into silence. Evidently, he was Cousin Cleo's husband.

Judy and Holly stood there. No one had invited them to sit down. Finally Diana, who hadn't spoken a word thus far, turned to her mother and said timidly, "Aren't you going to ask the girls if they've had breakfast, Mamma?"

"Thank you, Diana, but we've eaten—"

"I should hope so," Aunt Florence interrupted before Holly could finish. "It's nearly time for lunch."

"Please let us fix it. We'd love to," Judy offered quickly.

Alone in the kitchen, Judy plied Holly with questions about her sister. She felt she couldn't play the part of Doris without knowing a little more about her.

"Do I really look like Doris?" Judy asked.

Holly turned from the cupboard where she was

searching for canned goods while Judy put on water for coffee.

"I'm not sure. Her hair is like yours," Holly replied. "I don't know about her face. I haven't seen Doris in seven years, but neither have they."

"Then why in the world did they jump to the conclusion that I was Doris?" Judy asked.

Holly shrugged her shoulders.

"People do remember red hair, and I guess they had it figured out that if I did write and beg Doris to come and get me out of camp, she would do it. Maybe she'll come anyway if she reads about Uncle David's death."

"That *will* make it nice for me. Obviously, there can't be two of us. How long am I supposed to play this little game with your relatives?" Judy asked.

"Only until we find out what they were hunting for, and who dreamed up this reunion in the first place and why, and where Uncle David's son has been all these years that he never got in touch with his father, and what the real trouble was—"

"And about a million more things, I suppose? I see where I spend the rest of my life being Doris," declared Judy, giggling.

"Look!" Holly exclaimed, producing a glass jar filled with big slices of chicken cooked with noodles. "How about this for lunch? With a can of peas it will make a whole meal."

"Perfect," agreed Judy.

The relatives, however, did not think so. It turned out that they were not easy to please, especially Cousin Cleo.

"David must have put this chicken up himself," she commented at table. "It wants more salt."

"That was our fault," Judy apologized, passing the salt shaker.

She and Holly had worked hard to make the meal as attractive as possible, but they were glad when it was over.

Meanwhile, the sky had cleared and Judy suggested going for the suitcases.

"You are going to ask us to stay, aren't you?" she questioned the relatives.

"I don't know where you'll sleep," Cousin Cleo snapped. "Florence and Diana have one of the bedrooms and Fred and I have the other. The third one's being reserved for David's son, Clyde, who should be here before long. If Arlene comes, I'm afraid she'll have to sleep in the attic."

"Can't we sleep in the attic until she gets here?" Holly asked.

Cousin Cleo turned to Holly's aunt Florence.

"What do you think?"

But before Aunt Florence could answer, Diana said, "You'll have to let them stay, Mamma. Where else would they go?"

It was not a very cordial invitation, but Holly accepted it.

"I'm sure we'll be very comfortable in the attic," she said.

Cousin Fred gave her a searching look.

"Maybe more comfortable than we are on the second floor," he said, and then left the room abruptly.

There was an awkward silence. Then Diana said timidly, "There may be queer noises in the attic, too."

"Queer noises?" Holly echoed, looking from one of her relatives to the other.

"What sort of noises?" asked Judy.

"Well, to tell you the truth, it sounded like someone chuckling—or moaning. We couldn't make out which it was," Cousin Cleo admitted. "The sounds came from the other bedroom. The one I told you we were reserving for your uncle David's son, Clyde. Maybe he can get the door open. The room's locked tight, and so far we haven't been able to find the key."

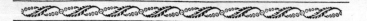

CHAPTER VII

The Ghost of David Potter

"So THAT's what they were looking for!" Judy exclaimed when she and Holly were finally on their way to the stalled car.

Judy had no difficulty in starting it now. The mud puddles in the road had dried out in the warm sunshine. It had turned out to be a beautiful day after all.

"We'll go to my house first," Judy announced as she and Holly started off. "It may seem a long way by the road, but we can cut through the pasture when we walk back. As the crow flies, your uncle was really our nearest neighbor."

"You must have known him quite well then."

Judy shook her head slowly.

"Nobody knew your uncle well, Holly. He was a

strange man. I liked him, but I never pretended to understand him. Sometimes he seemed perfectly happy, but at other times, there was a look in his face as if—as if someone had hurt him deeply."

"The relatives," Holly said bitterly. "They did everything in their power to make him miserable when he was alive. And now that he's dead I'm sure this reunion will turn out to be nothing more than a scramble to see who will get his property. I suppose there is a will—unless they've destroyed it."

"What would be their purpose in doing that?" asked Judy. "If he didn't leave a will, everything will go to his son—"

"It will? But that's terrible!" Holly exclaimed. "He doesn't deserve a cent. If he'd cared anything about his father, he would have showed up long before this. Judy, we simply have to find the will before he gets here."

"Your relatives may know where it is. They may have been searching the house for something besides that key," Judy said thoughtfully. "Do you think your uncle might have told one of your older sisters what he intended to do with his property?"

"I'll write and ask them," Holly decided. "I'll have to tell Doris about you anyway, in case she does come before we've finished looking into things. She's a counselor at a summer camp in northern California, but the camp will be closing soon. She teaches arts and crafts. She's really good at it," Holly added loyally.

"Oh, so she's artistic. Maybe I could get her an art job where Peter's sister works in Farrington," Judy suggested.

"Do you think you could? Then I'll write and tell her. I know she'd come if I begged her to. I've never asked her, because the trip costs so much," Holly explained. "But now it's different."

"Because of your uncle's death?" asked Judy.

"Yes. It sounds callous to say it, but he's sure to have left us something, maybe even his house."

"You wouldn't mind living in it, would you?" asked Judy. "I was half tempted to give myself away and ask you to stay at my house when your relatives mentioned those queer noises, but then I thought better of it. I'd rather like to help investigate them myself."

Holly smiled.

"I thought you would. It sounds like Bluebeard's chamber, doesn't it? Maybe when we open the locked room we'll find someone hanging by the hair—"

"We're more apt to find bats, or perhaps a pigeon that's flown in through the window. Pigeons do moan and chuckle. Anyway, they sound like that," Judy added. "I don't suppose anyone looked to see if a window was open."

"We'll look when we go back. It's funny that the relatives are all so jittery, isn't it?" asked Holly.

"Maybe their consciences are beginning to hurt—"

"If they have any," Holly broke in. "You'd actually think the house was haunted, the way they act."

" 'All houses wherein men have lived and died are haunted,' " Judy said.

She had stopped the car in front of her own house, but she was still sitting with her hands on the steering wheel, thoughtfully staring into space. Holly gave her a puzzled look.

"What was that?" she asked.

Judy laughed.

"I was just quoting something. I told you my brother scared me with it—or tried to. Now it seems a little funny. If all houses are haunted, what are we worrying about?"

"It's the relatives who are worrying. I'm not," declared Holly as she stepped out of the car and ran around to the side of the house to look at Judy's garden.

As Judy watched her running from one flower bed to the other and exclaiming over the flowers, the thought came to her that Holly was being deliberately gay to keep from showing how badly she really felt. Her uncle's death had been a great blow to her, Judy knew, but she had not shed a single tear.

"This is not the happy scene it appears to be," thought Judy, joining her in the garden.

The garden itself was certainly a cheerful place. Judy had placed her "mystic ball," souvenir of another mystery, in the center with a circular bed around it.

The garden was laid out in formal style with pebble paths. Now, in late summer, it was a riot of color. Phlox, zinnias and dahlias were all in bloom, and everywhere the sweet alyssum Judy and her little boarder had planted edged the flower beds with snowy white.

"It's beautiful! Beautiful! I can see you're an artistic person," Holly declared. "Wouldn't I love to plant a garden like this on that weedy lot beside Uncle David's house! The house is homelike inside, isn't it? I mean, it would be if—"

She stopped, listening a moment. Then she asked, "Judy, is anybody else here?"

"Only Blackberry."

The cat had come out to greet them. Judy introduced him and made him give Holly his paw. Then she picked him up and they all went inside.

"Oh, how lovely!" Holly exclaimed, looking around. "Judy, your home is like Uncle David's, only brighter and more cheerful looking. I could—"

"What could you do?" asked Judy when Holly hesitated.

"So much!" She clasped her hands. "I don't suppose there's a chance that Uncle David left his house to me, but if he did I could make it every bit as beautiful as yours."

"You couldn't live there all alone," Judy reminded her.

"Alone?" Holly seemed surprised. "Am I ever, with my head full of story people? I told you I wanted to be a writer, didn't I? That house would give me just the atmosphere I need. I'd be rich and famous in no time. Of course," she added more sensibly, "I'd have to have someone to work the farm. Maybe Eric would do it. He's Ruth's husband. They're always talking about the farm they're going to have some day. Eric doesn't like his job in the city. I met him once. He's nice. I think he's Danish. Anyway, he talks with an accent. Aunt Flo calls him 'that foreigner!' she added, giggling.

Holly ran on and on, talking of Ruth and Doris and exclaiming over Judy's house.

And while Holly talked, she and Judy packed a few of Judy's things and most of Holly's belongings in two smaller suitcases. "Otherwise the relatives will wonder why Doris came without a suitcase," Judy explained.

Also at Judy's suggestion, Holly removed her letters and what jewelry she possessed from her big suitcase and left them in the secret drawer of Judy's dresser for safekeeping.

Holly thought it was exciting to have a dresser with a secret drawer.

"Where did you get it?" she asked Judy.

"I bought it. Mother and Dad let me pick out my bedroom furniture myself. I was just about your age," Judy remembered. "It was right after the Roulsville flood. All our furniture was destroyed when the house was swept away. We had to buy new."

"I simply love new furniture," declared Holly, looking around her.

They returned to the living room with the two small suitcases. It was a pretty room, especially in the late afternoon when the sun was shining in through the west windows. But here the furniture was anything but new.

"This is mostly what Grandma left me," Judy explained.

"In her will?" Holly questioned.

Judy nodded. Again she had the feeling that her grandmother might disapprove of some of the changes she had made in the room. She decided to rehang a few of the old pictures. Perhaps even the mottoes. There was one, "Overcome Evil With Good," that seemed to belong beside the front door.

"There! How do you like it?" Judy asked when she had found it and set back in its old place.

Holly looked up from the typewriter. She was pounding out her letter to Doris by the "hunt-and-hit-'em" method. The typewriter was still in the bay window where Judy had left it. A shaft of sunlight coming in through the window behind her picked out the golden lights in Holly's brown hair and made it pretty. And Judy had thought it a drab color!

Holly's eyes were dreamy. Apparently she had not heard Judy's question.

"I could use that room back of the living room for a study. It would be as sunny and cheerful as this, wouldn't it?" she asked.

"You're still dreaming of what you might do with your uncle's house, aren't you?" Judy questioned.

"Yes," said Holly softly. "If Uncle David did remember me in his will and if—but why talk about it?" she broke off. "They'll get their hands on his property, I know. That's what they're here for. What was it you were saying, Judy?"

"I was pointing out this motto I just hung. How do you like it?"

Holly read it aloud. Then she smiled.

"It might work at that," she said. "I think I'll try it on the relatives."

Judy was waiting for her to finish her letter to Doris. She had already written a card to Ruth.

"I'll drop them both in our mailbox," Judy offered.

"Just a minute and I'll be through. I want to ask Doris one more thing. I wish I knew more about wills," Holly said thoughtfully.

"I can tell you something about them," Judy replied.

"Well, where are they kept, then?"

Judy laughed.

"I'm afraid I can't answer that one. Usually a lawyer helps draw a will, and if he doesn't keep it in his files he knows where it can be found. Or the witnesses may know. A will has to be witnessed by two people who are not related to the testator—"

"The who?"

"The one who is making the will. I learned all these legal terms from Peter," Judy explained. "He studied law. Maybe he helped your uncle draw up his will. He didn't say anything to me about it, though. The chances are that your uncle knew enough about law to write his will himself."

"But he'd still have to have witnesses, wouldn't he?" Holly asked.

"Yes. I should think he'd probably have asked his neighbors. Maybe the Absons witnessed his will. Anyway," Judy finished, "it would do no harm to ask them."

"Let's do it then. Uncle David must have made a will. He was fond of all three of us girls. And I'd so love to live in his house—"

"What's the matter?" asked Judy as Holly broke off suddenly.

Holly shivered.

"I don't know," she admitted, "but the strangest feeling came over me almost as if—as if we weren't alone in the house."

"We aren't," Judy said, trying to make light of it

although she knew the feeling, too. "Blackberry's still here. Maybe he sneezed or something."

Holly laughed, but she still looked a little uneasy.

"Don't you go imagining ghosts just because I did," Judy scolded.

And she told Holly about the transparent form she had seen in the garden, that looked so like her grandmother, and how, afterwards, she had seemed to feel her grandmother's disapproval of the changes that had been made in the house.

"I was sitting at the typewriter just as you are now," Judy added. "It must have been just about this time yesterday—"

"Judy!" Holly's voice was a scream. "I do see a transparent form! But it isn't your grandmother. It's my uncle David!"

CHAPTER VIII

Escape

For a minute the two girls were frozen, too frightened to move or speak. Judy had seen the transparent form, too. There could be no doubt about it. David Potter had appeared, like a ghost, in the same spot where Judy had seen what certainly looked like her grandmother the day before. Then he had vanished as mysteriously as he had appeared.

"It was his spirit!" Holly whispered at last. "Judy, let's get out of here. Let's take the suitcases and run—"

"Where?" asked Judy. "Do you imagine it will be any more pleasant in your uncle's house?"

"There it's—it's only noises," Holly sobbed. "It isn't anything—supernatural."

Judy wanted to say, "Neither was this," but such a

60

statement would require an explanation, and she had none. It had been strange enough to see the apparition yesterday. Seeing a ghostly David Potter had really unnerved her.

As she and Holly hurried through the pasture toward the Potter house, Judy could only say, "If I could just think how it happened . . . how it could happen! Real people aren't transparent. There must be some explanation!"

"You haven't seen any real people," Holly reminded her. "You have only seen people who are dead."

That was no comfort. The two girls hurried on in silence. They had reached the other side of the pasture and were just about to climb under the fence when a voice stopped them.

"Running to catch a train?" it said. "I see you've got your suitcases."

Judy whirled around. There stood her neighbor, Waldo Abson. She had never particularly liked him. Now her dislike for him grew. He was rubbing his chin and chuckling as if the sight of the two hurrying girls amused him greatly.

"What's so funny?" Judy asked, not too politely.

"So you're Doris Potter, eh, here from California?" Waldo Abson drawled.

He knew very well who Judy was. He must have been talking with Holly's relatives. Judy hoped he had not given her away. Somehow, from the way he was looking at her, she didn't believe he had.

His gaze shifted to Holly.

"And this is David Potter's youngest niece, or so they tell me. I'd like to ask one question. Are *any* of his relatives genuine?"

Holly faced him squarely, appearing much bolder than she really was.

"I am," she stated. "Don't you remember me?"

"Can't say that I do," he answered gruffly, after peering intently into her eyes for a moment.

"You are Mr. Abson, aren't you?" Holly asked.

He nodded, still watching her.

"I thought so. I recognized you right away. You and my father and Uncle David and another man whose name I don't remember used to call yourselves the Dry Brook Hollow quartet."

"North Hollow quartet," he corrected her. "That's Dry Brook Hollow the other side of the hill. You two girls were running down it as if something was after you. What's the matter, Judy? Did old Daisy turn on you?"

"He knows you!" Holly gasped.

"Of course he does. He's one of our nearest neighbors. But he hasn't told your relatives who I am. Have you, Mr. Abson?"

He shook his head.

"Not yet," he said significantly.

"Please don't," begged Holly, ignoring the look of suspicion in the old farmer's eyes. "We need your help. We intended to stop by and see you some time today. There are some questions we want to ask you."

"Well, fire away!"

Holly began by asking a few cautious questions about her uncle, and was told that he had liked to live alone and mind his own business—and that his relatives would do well to follow his example.

"Are you sure he preferred living alone?" Holly questioned anxiously.

"That's what he said."

"He didn't mean it, though. I'm sure he didn't," Holly insisted. "Now there's just one more question I'd like to ask and then I won't bother you any more. It's about my uncle's will."

"Never heard he had made one," Waldo Abson retorted. This time his voice was so unpleasant that Holly backed away from him and grasped Judy's hand for reassurance.

"You won't—you won't give Judy away?" she asked, beginning to tremble. "I asked her to be Doris. I came here alone and I—I'm frightened. I need her help."

Judy's neighbor chuckled at that.

"Your 'sister' is supposed to be the neighborhood ghost chaser, but from the way she ran down the hill it looked as if it was the other way around."

"It was," Judy admitted. "We really were frightened."

"You were, eh? Well, Judy or Doris, whichever you want to call yourself, I don't know what you're up to, but I'll play along with you awhile, for the sake of your grandmother. God rest her soul! As for this other girl, she'd better be the real Holly Potter. Seems to me I do remember a skinny kid about half her size. Her uncle was real fond of her, too. Wanted to keep her. My wife even offered to do his housekeeping and mother all three of the little orphans. But their high and mighty relatives wouldn't hear of it. David Potter was too poor!"

"He isn't now."

"*Wasn't,*" her neighbor corrected Judy sharply, "but he was then. And so, instead of leaving the kids here where they could breathe good country air and watch things grow the way they ought to, they were snatched off and separated against their wishes. Oh, I knew about it! I knew plenty. I told David his little Christmas girl, as he used to call the youngest one, would be just as greedy and selfish as the rest of them before Cleo got through with her, and I wasn't far wrong." He glared at Holly and fired his parting shot at her directly. "So already you want to know what your uncle did with his will, eh?"

"It—it doesn't matter," Holly stammered. "Come on, Judy, let's go."

"If you're headed for your uncle's house, I wouldn't be in too big a hurry if I were you," Waldo Abson warned her. "He always used to declare up and down that if his relatives fought over his property after he was dead, he'd come back and haunt them. And David Potter was a man of his word!"

With this final bombshell, he turned abruptly toward his own farm while the two girls stared after him in utter bewilderment. For fully a minute neither of them spoke. Holly was the first to recover her powers of speech.

"Judy, am I—am I greedy and selfish the way he said?"

Judy shook her head slowly.

"You don't seem so to me. You didn't come to fight over your uncle's property, that's certain, because you came before you knew he was dead."

"So did the others," Holly said. "They wanted to make up to him because they thought he'd leave them some of his money when he did die. But I didn't. I—I just wanted to see him. I wanted to put my arms around his neck and tell him I loved him and ask him to sing the way he used to. He was always so glad when I asked him to sing. His eyes would light up— Oh, Judy!" she broke off. "They *were* hurt when he looked at me. Does he think I'm greedy, too?"

Judy didn't know how to answer Holly's question. She had recognized the hurt expression, too.

"It *was* David Potter. I know it. And yet how could he appear transparent? How could he appear at all, when he's dead?" Judy thought. Aloud she said, "Holly, I don't understand it any better than I did before. But at least we can watch Waldo Abson and see what he's up to. He may have an eye on the property himself. I don't believe he never heard of a will. If he didn't witness it, he's probably one of the beneficiaries. He knows something, that's certain. He may even know something about what we saw."

"Our faces would tell him we saw something! We must look awful," Holly added. "I feel as if every drop of color had drained out of my face. You're pale, too, Judy."

"I'm not so much frightened now as I am angry. Mr. Abson makes me angry," declared Judy. "He's up to something. I don't know what, but I'll find out. If he thinks, just because we're girls, he can stand there and make fun of us—"

"He *was* making fun of us, wasn't he? Just the same," Holly said, "I don't believe he'd really trick us. He and my uncle were good friends. Why, he said once in one of his letters that Waldo Abson was the only true friend he had left. That was when he wrote and told me that your grandparents had died. I can't help feeling that it is the rest of us who have hurt him."

"You haven't, Holly."

"I'm not so sure. I can't seem to forget that pained look in his eyes. It was the very look you described, and he was looking right at me."

"I know," Judy said. "I wish I understood it. Maybe there's a clue in that poem Horace quoted after all. He started to say something about 'the spirit world around this world of sense,' but I made him stop because Peter had objected. Now I wish I hadn't. Holly, Horace *knew* there was going to be a 'haunted house' around here somewhere. He said it would make a good newspaper story. How did Horace know?"

"Maybe he saw something, too," Holly suggested.

They were approaching the Potter house. Judy stopped a minute to look at it speculatively before they turned up the walk. Was this the house Horace meant, or was it her own?

"I'll ask him about it tomorrow," she decided. "I'm too tired to think about it any more today. Horace wouldn't explain anything, anyway. He'd just tease. If he doesn't stop it he's going to be as exasperating as Waldo Abson by the time he's his age."

Judy sighed as another thought came to her. "By then I'll be an old lady, too," she said. "I've never thought much about getting old and dying, but wouldn't it be strange if we didn't really leave this earth at all? I mean," she added, laughing a little, "if our spirits were still around—"

"I've often thought they were," Holly broke in.

"Sometimes my parents seem so very near. Once I woke up suddenly when the first streak of light was coming in my window, and I thought I saw them. They were just standing there as if they'd stepped into my room for a moment to bless me. It wasn't frightening, like seeing Uncle David. It was more like a dream."

"It was a dream."

"I suppose so," Holly sighed. "But it seemed so real. I don't believe anyone else could have seen them, though. It was probably only my imagination."

"That's what really puzzles me," declared Judy. "I probably imagined Grandma, too. But we wouldn't both imagine we saw your uncle."

Holly shook her head.

"It's because they buried him in Florida. I told you he'd never rest."

"Well, I will," declared Judy, dismissing this superstition before they entered the house. "Ghost or no ghost, I'm going to sleep tonight."

CHAPTER IX

A Pledge of Friendship

JUDY found her resolution hard to keep. After an unpleasant meal with the relatives, she and Holly were shown to their attic room. It was hot and stuffy. Even with all the windows open the air still seemed close.

"Maybe it will cool off after a little," Judy said hopefully.

"Let's go for a walk until it does, then," Holly suggested. "I forgot to mail my letter and postcard."

The walk to the mailbox was pleasant. It was dark outside now, but Judy had brought her flashlight so the girls had no difficulty in seeing their way. The messages to Holly's two sisters were soon safely mailed.

On the way back from the mailbox the two girls

talked over the events of the day. Nothing seemed to make sense.

Even Judy, who was usually the first to suggest a possible solution, had to admit that she was completely baffled.

"This is one mystery I'm going to let Horace help solve if he can," she declared.

"Let's not think about it any more," Holly suggested. "We won't sleep a wink tonight if we do, and I'm tired."

Judy was tired, too. She suggested going up to their attic room as soon as they returned to the house, but Holly thought they ought to do a little exploring first.

"I'm curious about that room with the two doors leading in at the end of the living room," she admitted.

"The one you said you might use for a study?" Judy questioned.

"Yes. Let's search it. I could tell from the talk around the dinner table that something's missing. It may be the key to the locked room, or it may be Uncle David's will. But, whatever it is, I'd like to be the one to find it."

"It might establish you in the good graces of your relatives at that," Judy agreed. "They're bound to find out I'm not Doris before very much longer. Then you'll be on your own."

"The thought scares me. What'll I do? Where will I live?" asked Holly.

"There's a spare bedroom in my house. I can't keep on being your sister," Judy said, "but I can be your friend."

Holly looked at Judy to see if she really meant that. It was too dark for her to see the older girl's face, but the reassuring pressure of Judy's hand on hers told her that she did.

"You're certainly a friend in need. I never had a friend like you," Holly declared. "Really, Judy, I feel closer to you in one day than I did to any of the girls in boarding school in all the time I was there. Most of them needed friends, too, but instead of being friends, they just picked on each other. If I have to go back—"

"What?" asked Judy when Holly hesitated.

"I was just thinking I might be more of a friend myself, and then maybe I'd make friends. Like you, Judy. But I don't want to go back. I came here intending to stay. It isn't greedy of me to hope Uncle David provided a home for me in his will, is it?"

Holly looked longingly at his house as they turned up the walk.

"It's so near your house. We could be friends and do things together when Peter's away—"

"Yes, and when he's here. It would be nice to have you for a neighbor," Judy agreed. "You'd like Peter, too, and you'd adore his sister. All my friends could be your friends and you'd make new friends of your own, too. I think you've learned how to do it already."

"From you," Holly said gratefully.

Then, suddenly, both girls laughed. "What are we standing here for?" they asked each other. "Let's go in."

As they entered the house a strange feeling came over Judy. She felt compelled to whisper, as if for fear of disturbing someone, although there seemed to be no one on the lower floor.

The living room was deserted. Judy noted how similar it was to her own living room, even to the clock on the mantel. The room was furnished just as she remembered it, Holly declared, except for a new grand piano which looked oddly out of place. The chairs were mostly rockers, which had been drawn up before the fireplace. No one was sitting in them now. Apparently Holly's relatives had retired to their rooms early. At first the girls could hear no sound at all in the house. But outside, the wind was rising, and its whispering in the trees was almost like a voice.

"Hear it!" Holly whispered, stopping still in the middle of the living room to listen. "Doesn't it remind you of someone singing? Uncle David wrote a song about the wind:

" *'Then sing to the winds as merry as they,*
  A song for the man who works his way.' "

"Don't sing it," begged Judy. "The wind doesn't sound merry tonight. It sounds sad."

"Almost as if it were moaning," Holly agreed. "Judy!" she gasped, clutching Judy's arm. "*Is* that the wind? It's more like—organ music! Uncle David used to have an organ—right here in this room—just where that big piano stands now."

"Maybe it's in there!"

Judy walked over to one of the two doors at the end of the living room and tapped lightly on the oak panel. When no one answered, she swung open the door. The room was quite dark.

Still mystified, Judy groped for the electric switch. She found it right by the door. When she pressed the button, a soft yellow ceiling light threw its beams into every corner of the room.

"That's strange," she whispered. "I was sure the music came from this room, but there's no organ here."

"Oh, how lovely!" Holly exclaimed, following Judy into the room. "I remember it now. Uncle David called it the library, but I thought it was bigger than this."

It was a small room. Probably it had been a porch when the house was first built, as it was long and narrow. One entire wall was lined with bookshelves. Windows were on the other three sides of the room. A desk, a chair and a single cot were the only other furnishings.

"If we're going to search the house, this would be a

good place to start," declared Judy. "Your uncle may have kept his important papers in this desk."

She began pulling open the desk drawers, one by one. To her surprise, they were all empty. Holly looked in a large wastepaper basket.

"Even this is empty," she declared. "There isn't a scrap of paper anywhere."

"Then they probably did find the will," Judy decided. "Your uncle undoubtedly made a fair division of his property. I'm sure your other relatives will respect his wishes, so let's forget it and go up to bed."

"Oh, Judy! Not yet," begged Holly. "We did hear something. If it wasn't organ music then it must have been that moaning Cousin Cleo said she heard. Maybe it's only the wind, but if it's so spooky down here, what's it going to be like in that stuffy old attic? At least this room is cool."

"The cot's too narrow for both of us," observed Judy, "but if you want to sleep there—"

"Alone? Oh, no!" Holly objected.

She had forgotten the story people she had said were such good company. Judy laughed.

"I thought you were never alone. That's what you told me."

"Oh, but I am! I was the loneliest girl in the whole world before I met you," confessed Holly. "If we're really friends, let's stay together."

"You could sleep on the cot. I'd rest well enough

on the living-room sofa. There'd only be a wall between us," Judy said.

"Even that's too much. You know, Judy," Holly added, looking around her, "the living room would be light enough if these two doors were left open. I mean in the daytime. I wonder why they were closed."

"Your cousin Fred was in here when we first arrived," Judy remembered. "Maybe he was reading and wanted to shut out the noise the rest of your relatives were making. There are a lot of books in here."

"We really ought to look through each one of them," declared Holly. "Uncle David used to keep things in his Bible. Maybe that's where he put his will."

"There doesn't seem to be any Bible here, but look!"

Judy pounced upon a fat volume and began searching through it so eagerly that Holly asked, "What in the world have you found?"

"Longfellow's poems! Every one of them!" Judy announced triumphantly. "Ah, here's what I was looking for."

"Why, it's 'Haunted Houses'!" exclaimed Holly when Judy pointed out the poem. "That's the one you said your brother quoted, isn't it? Let's take the book upstairs with us. It won't be missed."

Judy agreed.

"I'm sure it must hold a clue," she commented as they passed through the living room on their way upstairs.

Again there came a sound like faint organ music from the room they had just left. But this time both girls were ready to believe it was only the wind.

CHAPTER X

Ghostly Music

"There it is again! It's louder up here."

Holly stopped dead still at the top of the stairs and listened. It did seem to be louder. Then it stopped and the house was even quieter than before.

"Sh! Everybody seems to be asleep," Judy whispered as they tiptoed past the three closed doors in the upstairs hall.

A fourth door led to the attic. The stairs creaked as they went up.

"This house scares me," Holly admitted. "We still don't know which one of those doors is locked or what made that sound like organ music. Remember those queer noises Diana mentioned?"

"Your cousin Cleo said it sounded like chuckling—"

77

"Or moaning," Holly added, beginning to undress.

Judy was sitting on the edge of the bed with the book in her lap.

"It says here that ghosts are quiet—and harmless," she laughed.

"Read it, Judy," urged Holly. "I love to hear poetry read aloud."

Judy hesitated.

"You may not love to hear this. I'm not sure it's a good idea to read it just before you go to bed. It may keep you awake."

"I'd stay awake wondering what it said if you didn't read it," Holly declared. "So let's have it. If you don't want to read it aloud, I will."

"Let's take turns," Judy suggested. "First you read a verse and then I will. And while we're reading we'll look for clues."

"All right," said Holly. And she began to read:

" '*All houses wherein men have lived and died
Are haunted houses. Through the open doors
The harmless phantoms on their errands glide,
With feet that make no sound upon the floors.*"

"There! I told you it said ghosts are quiet and harmless. Nothing, really. And yet, if they are nothing, how does Longfellow think you can meet them?" asked Judy. "The second verse says:

" 'We meet them at the doorway, on the stair,
    Along the passages they come and go,
    Impalpable impressions on the air,
    A sense of something moving to and fro.'

"That's what I felt in my house," she added when she had finished reading the verse, "a sense of something coming in from the garden with me—but I'm sure it was only a gust of wind."

"You never can be sure of things you feel like that," Holly said earnestly.

"Maybe you're right," Judy agreed lightly. "Sometimes I'm not even sure of things I see."

"Me either. It says 'impalpable impressions on the air.' Doesn't that sound like a clue?" asked Holly. "It was a sort of—well, a sort of impression we saw, wasn't it? Does impalpable mean transparent?"

"I don't think so. More likely, intangible. We could look it up in the dictionary. I suppose there is one downstairs."

"No, Judy! Stay with me," Holly protested. "We can look it up tomorrow. Let's go on reading now. I like this poem. The next verse says:

" 'There are more guests at table than the hosts
    Invited—' "

Holly broke off, giggling. "You know, that's true! I mean, there are more people here than Uncle David invited. He didn't invite me. I wonder why?" She sighed.

"Perhaps he had a reason," Judy said quietly.

"Perhaps," agreed Holly as she continued:

> " '—*The illuminated hall*
> *Is thronged with quiet, inoffensive ghosts,*
> *As silent as the pictures on the wall.*' "

Judy shivered, remembering another mystery, *The Living Portrait*. That picture had been silent, too. Still, she was glad it no longer hung over the fireplace in her own house to torment her.

Holly handed her the book.

"Your turn," she said a little drowsily.

She lay back on her pillow and closed her eyes as Judy began:

> " '*The stranger at my fireside cannot see*
> *The forms I see, nor hear the sounds I hear—*' "

"Judy! *I* hear something!" cried Holly, wide awake again and sitting straight up in bed to listen. "It—it is organ music. I'm sure of it."

Judy put down the book and listened, too. Where it was coming from, she couldn't imagine, but it did sound like organ music. A familiar strain from one of David Potter's own compositions stole through the house, rising in volume and then falling away. This time Judy knew it was not the wind.

"You say your uncle did have an organ?" she asked Holly thoughtfully.

"Yes. It used to be in the living room, but it's gone now," the younger girl answered.

Judy was thinking fast. The music could have come from the room above them when they were in the library. Now it sounded directly below them.

"Maybe the organ was moved to the second floor," she suggested.

"Maybe," agreed Holly with a shiver. "But who would be playing it in the middle of the night like this? The house is all dark. There wasn't a beam of light from any of the windows when we came in. I took particular notice."

"There may be now." Judy spoke reassuringly although she did not feel as brave as she sounded. "It's quite possible one of your relatives became restless and got up to play the organ."

"I don't believe it," declared Holly. "None of them can play a note."

"Then there must be someone else in the house. I'm still dressed. I think I'll have a look around," Judy declared. "Something very strange is going on, and I don't like it."

She started toward the stairs.

"Wait! I want to go with you," begged Holly.

She was dressing as quickly as she could.

As Judy waited she tried to locate the music.

"It could be coming from the second floor," she decided. "That's a difficult piece of music, too. Only an accomplished musician could play it like that."

"Uncle David was an accomplished musician," Holly said uneasily.

Judy turned to look at her.

"Holly! You don't actually believe it's his ghost, do you?"

"I—I don't know," Holly faltered. "We saw something, didn't we? It—it might have been his spirit. It must have been, because it—it was transparent. Maybe I might get used to the idea of Uncle David's spirit coming back here and playing. It was only that look on his face that frightened me. If I could just see him and explain things—"

"What things?" asked Judy.

"The way I feel. I never told him how much I loved his music. He always said it would live longer than he would. Do you think he intended to come back and play it?"

Judy shivered.

"I hope not," she answered. "Good music always lives longer than the people who write it. That is, if other people play it. And someone else is certainly playing your uncle's music now."

"But singing it with *his* voice!" Holly exclaimed. "Listen!"

As Judy listened, she fancied she, too, could hear a man's voice singing. Then the words became clearer.

"*Wanting too much! Wanting too much!*
Says I to myself, there are many of such
Whose trouble in life is
They're wanting too much."

"It *is* Uncle David!" exclaimed Holly. "I know it!"

"Oh, Holly, it can't be!" Judy protested. "It's just a good imitation."

"It's the real thing," declared Holly. "Let's go down."

Pulling a dress over her head and fastening it on the way, she followed Judy down the narrow attic stairs.

The music had stopped by the time they reached the second floor. The three doors were tightly closed. Not a glimmer of light came from underneath them.

"Where was it?" Holly whispered.

"Wait!" advised Judy.

And so the two girls waited shivering and huddling together in the darkness until the mysterious music began again. It was the same tune.

"Oh, Judy! Do *I* want too much?" Holly asked.

"Sh!" Judy cautioned her.

But it was too late. Down the hall a door flew open. A light flashed on and Cousin Cleo's head, decorated with curling papers, appeared.

"What's going on?" she asked sharply. "Where is that music coming from?"

"We don't know," Judy replied. "That's what we came down here to find out. There isn't an organ in your room, is there?"

Cousin Cleo straightened herself and snorted, "Certainly not!"

"There must be one somewhere on this floor," Judy said reasonably. "What about that room across from yours?"

"That's Aunt Florence's room. She and Diana are probably sleeping—"

"We *were* sleeping, you mean. Nobody could sleep with this racket going on," declared Holly's aunt, who had flung open her door.

Behind her Diana peered out like a ghost herself. She did not venture out into the hall. The music swelled louder and louder.

"It's coming from that room!" declared Judy, darting to the end of the hall and placing her ear against the door.

The music ceased abruptly.

"But that's the locked room," Aunt Flo protested. "We told you we couldn't find the key. Nobody can get in—"

"Except a ghost," Diana chattered. "Mamma, let's leave. This house is haunted. I wouldn't want to live here even if Uncle David did leave it to us."

"Humph!" her mother snorted. "I suppose you wouldn't want any part of the royalties from his gas well either, would you? Diana! You're white as a sheet and shivering from head to foot. Go back to bed!" Aunt Flo added, "We've probably scared the ghost away—if it was a ghost, which I very much doubt."

"I doubt it myself," declared Judy. "The organ must be in that room and someone alive is in there playing it. I think Holly and I will wait right here at the top of the stairs until whoever it is comes out."

"Suit yourselves," agreed Cousin Cleo. "The rest of us are going back to bed."

With that both doors closed. It was not until after the two girls had waited all of half an hour in the dimly lighted hall that Judy thought of something.

"Holly," she asked suddenly, "does your cousin Fred play the organ?"

"Not that I know of," the younger girl replied. "Why do you ask?"

"Well, *he* didn't come out to see what was going on. And when I went over to the door of the locked room I could tell it was locked from the inside. The key was in the keyhole. That's why we couldn't see any light coming through," declared Judy. "I was thinking that if there's another entrance to that room, and if your cousin Fred does play the organ, he could have gone in there. Maybe there's a connecting door between the two rooms. There could be."

"I suppose so," Holly agreed doubtfully. "Cousin Fred isn't exactly the type to play tricks, though."

"Just how does he feel about this family reunion?" Judy asked.

"Cousin Fred doesn't express his feelings. He's the silent type," Holly replied. "Usually he does whatever Cousin Cleo suggests to avoid arguments. He's really the one who's related to me, though. His father was Uncle David's oldest brother. My father was his youngest brother, and Aunt Flo was his sister. Until his son turned up, we were his nearest relatives."

"What about his wife?" asked Judy.

"Nobody knows what became of her after she divorced him and went back to Florida."

"Well," Judy yawned. "There's no use waiting here if there is a connecting door between those rooms. Let's get a little sleep and find out tomorrow."

Holly agreed. But before they were halfway up the attic stairs a loud noise directly below them drove all thought of sleep from their heads.

"What's that?" cried Holly, clutching Judy's arm to keep herself from falling. The noise had made her jump.

"I don't know, but I intend to find out," declared Judy. "It sounds like someone banging on the front door."

CHAPTER XI

Clyde

"Who can be arriving at this hour?" asked Holly, as the two girls hurried downstairs.

The clock on the mantel over the living-room fireplace told them it was exactly two o'clock. As the clock struck, the pounding on the door was repeated. Before unlocking the door, Judy peered cautiously through the glass.

"Who is it?" Holly whispered.

"I don't know," Judy replied. "It's too dark outside to see."

She opened the door.

The man standing outside was young and good looking. "Too good looking," was Judy's first thought. He was tall, fair-haired and fair-skinned,

87

with a fresh, pink complexion and a rather weak chin. He was certainly less terrifying than his knock.

"Hello!" he exclaimed, and added quickly, "I'm sorry to disturb you at this hour but I just got in. May I introduce myself? I'm Clyde Potter."

Judy was not surprised, although Holly seemed a little taken aback.

"Oh!" she exclaimed. "I didn't—that is, I thought you would be darker. All my father's relatives are dark."

"I'm the exception, I guess." The young man smiled disarmingly. "I presume you're my cousins or you wouldn't be here in my father's house."

"This is Doris," Holly said, introducing Judy. "I'm Holly. Come in, won't you? Shall I call you Cousin Clyde?"

"Clyde will be enough. Let's forget we're cousins and just be friends, shall we?"

He was looking at Judy as he spoke. She met his gaze coolly.

"How did you come?" she asked. "The midnight flyer doesn't stop at Roulsville."

"The Greyhound bus does. In fact, the driver very obligingly let me off right at the corner. It was only a short walk from there."

"It seemed long to us," declared Holly. "We had to walk it this morning in the rain."

"That was yesterday morning," Judy reminded her.

"It's nearly morning again. Cousin Clyde must be tired."

"I am at that," he admitted. "If you will just tell me where my room—"

His room! The thought hit both girls at the same time. It was locked! The mysterious organ music had been coming from there. Then Judy thought of the library. She explained the situation quickly and said she hoped he would be comfortable on the cot.

"Thanks, this is fine. I could sleep anywhere," Clyde replied, setting down his suitcase and looking around after Judy had showed him in. She thought he was looking with especial interest at the desk.

"He's going to be surprised to find all the desk drawers empty," she whispered later to Holly.

"Not as surprised as he will be if that organ starts playing again. I hope it doesn't," Holly added, "but if it does I'm just going to ignore it. I intend to sleep the rest of the night no matter what."

"Me, too," agreed Judy. "I'm going to need a clear head tomorrow. That is, if I don't wake up and find out that I dreamed this whole impossible adventure."

Holly giggled.

"You didn't dream me. Pinch me if you don't believe I'm real. Ouch!" she exclaimed as Judy took her at her word and gave her a playful pinch.

The two girls had returned to their attic room and were soon in bed, with the door to the attic securely bolted, although, as Holly pointed out, bolts and locks meant nothing to wandering spirits.

"I'm thinking of wandering relatives," Judy explained. "Until this mystery is solved, I'm not ready to trust anybody—"

"Not even me? I have been hiding something," Holly confessed, producing the volume of Longfellow's poems from under her pillow. "I read the whole poem your brother was quoting, and there isn't a clue in it. To tell you the truth, I rather like the idea of spirits the way the poet explains them."

"You do?" Judy was surprised. She turned on the light again to see for herself.

"I like this verse in particular," Holly pointed out. "It isn't wrong to want too much if you're willing to work for it. I'm sure it isn't. See, it says here:

" *'The spirit world around this world of sense*
Floats like an atmosphere, and everywhere
Wafts through these earthly mists and vapors dense
A vital breath of more ethereal air.' "

"There were no mists and vapors in the garden when we saw those—what we did see. It was bright sunlight," Judy remembered. "As for the ethereal air, we could do with a little real air up here in this attic."

"It isn't as hot as it was. I think I can sleep now," Holly added. "This poem actually has something soothing about it. I like what it says about our lives being kept in balance:

> " 'By opposite attractions and desires;
>   The struggle of the instinct that enjoys,
>   And the more noble instinct that aspires.'

"You know, Judy, it's really my more noble instinct that wants too much. I'm sure it is. I want to get things for myself—by writing. That's certainly a high aspiration. Too high, Cousin Cleo tells me. She disapproves of my scribbling, as she calls it, but Uncle David would be glad—*is* glad—" Holly's voice trailed off.

"You're thinking of that 'spirit world around this world of sense,' aren't you?" said Judy teasingly. "Longfellow probably got that idea from the Indians when he was doing the research for *Hiawatha*. The Indians are great believers in spirits. Invisible spirits, though, not transparent people wandering around in gardens and scaring people. That's certainly not Longfellow's idea of the spirit world, either."

"What is his idea?" Holly asked drowsily.

Judy thought about that for several minutes.

"I don't believe that poem was meant to make people superstitious," she replied finally. "It was just meant to explain their feelings about old houses where people have lived and died—houses people call haunted."

"Like this one?"

"Yes, and mine, too. I never expected to see Grandma, though. That doesn't fit, somehow. There must be someone who looks like her just a little—or who has a purple dress like hers."

"Somebody transparent?" asked Holly. "You can't see through real people."

"You can see through their reflections. It *must* have been somebody alive. I ought to be able to figure it out. I have an idea. Maybe we can try it out tomorrow. If we go back to my house, maybe—"

She stopped. Holly wasn't listening. She had rolled over on her side and was already asleep. Judy turned off the light again. She could reach the pull chain without getting out of bed, as it had a long tassel on the end.

For a little while she lay there in the dark, thinking. Holly was right. The poem did have a soothing effect on a person's nerves. Her problems soon forgotten, Judy slept soundly until morning. It was quite late when she awoke. Holly was already up and dressing.

"I meant to get downstairs ahead of the relatives to introduce Cousin Clyde," she explained when Judy asked her why she was hurrying. "I don't know what they'll think if they find him on the cot in the library. Cousin Fred seems to have appropriated that room for a daytime retreat—"

"And the locked room for a retreat at night. I did

figure out that much," declared Judy, hopping out of bed and hurrying into her clothes. She didn't want to be left out of the excitement.

A murmur of voices from downstairs told her it was too late for Holly to introduce Clyde Potter to her other relatives. They had already discovered him.

"I feel sorry for him," Holly confessed as they descended the stairs and the voices in the library became clearer. Apparently it was Holly's aunt Florence who had found the strange young man asleep on the cot.

"You say you are David Potter's son, but how do we know that?" she was demanding. "I don't suppose my two nieces asked for any proof. Your smile was enough. But I'm not so gullible."

"Will this do?" Clyde asked coldly, handing Aunt Florence a photostatic copy of his birth certificate and a photograph of himself when he was a baby. His father was holding him, and on the back of the picture it said, *David Potter with son Clyde, age three months.*

"Humph!" snorted Aunt Florence. "You don't expect me to recognize you from that picture, do you? All babies look alike."

"How about this one?"

Clyde was six in the photograph he now handed her.

"That's Mother with me," he explained. "She died a year ago. I've been meaning to get in touch with my father ever since. Mother talked against him, naturally, but I always had an idea I'd like him. The way things were, I couldn't very well see him while I was living with her. That is, without causing more trouble. This is her last picture."

"May I see it?" asked Judy.

The photographs were passed around.

"Am I supposed to know his mother?" Judy whispered, taking Holly aside.

"You probably wouldn't remember her. I don't," Holly whispered back. "Cousin Clyde must be about your age or maybe a little older. That is his mother's picture all right. Uncle David had a picture of her, and she looked just like that. He had a picture of Clyde when he was a baby, too."

"This picture?" asked Judy, looking at the first photograph Clyde had exhibited.

Holly nodded her head.

The other relatives who had gathered around him seemed satisfied with Clyde's proof of who he was, but not Aunt Florence. She still regarded him coldly.

"Well, if you are Clyde Potter, it's about time you arrived," she declared. "You say your mother's dead. Did she ever marry again?"

"Oh, yes. And my stepfather has always been very good to me. I still live with him in Florida," Clyde replied quickly.

"I'm sorry your real father wasn't here to make you welcome," Cousin Cleo put in, "but I suppose you did get acquainted."

"Yes, a little. My father wasn't an easy man to know. He was just beginning to warm up to me when—" He paused as if deeply affected by the memory of the train wreck.

"How did it happen?" Aunt Florence asked.

"Just as it was reported in the papers," Clyde replied. "We were in the dining car when the crash came. My father was thrown across the car so violently that he went right through a shattered window. It was horrible! Women were screaming all around us."

"How about the men? I suppose they kept quiet and played the part of heroes. You seem to have come through without a scratch," Aunt Florence observed.

"I was thrown underneath a table—"

"Then how could you see what happened to your father?"

"I didn't see it," Clyde confessed. "As a matter of fact, I blacked out for a minute. The shock, you know. I was told afterwards what had happened."

"When did you see your father?" Cousin Cleo questioned.

Clyde gulped and passed his hand across his forehead as if to erase the scene from his mind.

"Not until the next day when he was pulled out of the swamp," he said. "I did what I thought was right."

"Humph! What you thought!" sniffed Aunt Florence. "What about what he thought? He shouldn't have been buried in Florida. His spirit will never rest away from his own home."

Judy and Holly looked at each other.

"That's just what you said!" Judy exclaimed.

"And we did see him—"

"What's this?" demanded Cousin Cleo, whirling on them.

"It—it was probably only our imagination. But Doris and I thought we saw him. He was looking right at us as if—well, almost as if someone had hurt his feelings. I know it sounds impossible," Holly faltered, "but we could see right through him!" she finished with a shiver.

"Nonsense! We've heard strange noises, but there's no such thing as ghosts," snorted Aunt Florence.

"What sort of noises?" Clyde asked.

"You'll find out," Cousin Cleo warned him significantly as she motioned the assembled relatives out of the room.

CHAPTER XII

An Unfair Accusation

"I DIDN'T like the way they acted," declared Holly later, when she and Judy went into the kitchen. "I ought not to have told them what we saw. Naturally, they didn't believe us. Who would? What did Cousin Cleo mean, anyway?"

"No doubt she expects to hear the organ playing again," replied Judy. "I noticed that your cousin Fred was silent, as usual. He must be the organist. All the rest of them were out in the hall last night. I'm sure there must be a connecting door—"

"Sh!" cautioned Holly. "Here they come."

The kitchen was soon filled with hungry relatives. There was very little in the house to eat, as they shortly discovered. Waldo Abson, who had been taking care of the place ever since David Potter left, had placed a pail of milk and a basket of eggs just outside the back door, but there was nothing else except a little powdered coffee.

"Enough for two cups," Cousin Cleo judged, holding up the jar and peering through the glass.

Aunt Florence took a pad and pencil down from the wall and began flinging open cupboard doors and making a list of needed supplies. It looked as if she intended to stay.

"And why not?" she demanded when Cleo asked her about it. "If you think I'm going to let anybody else walk off with this property, you've got another think coming. I know my rights."

Clyde said nothing, but the look he gave her said very plainly that he also knew his.

Breakfast was hardly a cozy meal. Clyde left the house as soon as he had finished eating. Aunt Florence blamed Holly and Judy, or Doris, as she called her, for letting Clyde into the house in the first place.

"You know very well he's after your uncle's property," she charged. "He'll get it, too, if that will doesn't show up. I'm sure David would have cut him off with a dollar, but he wouldn't have forgotten his own sister—"

"Or his dead brother's only son," put in Cousin Cleo with a glance at the back door through which her husband had just departed.

"Wasn't there a thing among those papers, Mamma?" asked Diana.

Her mother looked at her reprovingly. But Judy seized the opportunity and asked, "What papers? I noticed the desk in the library was empty."

"Aha! So the nieces are searching for the will, too. I suspected as much," declared Cousin Cleo. "What with all that noise last night, I hardly slept a wink."

"Cousin Fred seems to have slept all right," Holly observed pointedly.

"He's a sound sleeper. He tells me he didn't even hear the organ music, and I believe him."

"He doesn't play the organ himself, does he?" Judy ventured.

"Fred? Play?" Cousin Cleo laughed. "Why, that man can't tell one note from another. No, it wasn't your cousin Fred who was playing and singing last night. You can be sure of that."

"It sounded like Uncle David himself," Diana began. "He composed that song. Nobody else can sing it the way he did."

"What about his son?" Cousin Cleo asked sharply.

"He didn't arrive until afterwards," declared Judy.

"Maybe he didn't, and maybe he did," sniffed Aunt Florence. "How do we know you didn't let him out of the locked room? Maybe the three of you are in this together. Why else would Holly have told us that wild tale about seeing your uncle's ghost? You want the rest of us to believe this house is haunted, don't you? Answer me! Don't you?"

The accusation left Judy speechless.

"Why, that's—that's ridiculous!" exclaimed Holly. "Why would we want people to think a thing like that?"

"To help that young impostor you let into the house. That's why," retorted Aunt Florence.

"He isn't an impostor. You saw his proof of who he is, and I think it's terrible the way everybody is treating him," Holly added. "After all, he is Uncle David's son and if there isn't a will—"

"There is! I'm sure of it. In fact," Aunt Florence admitted, "David told me he'd written one. I brought the letter with me, but when I looked for it this morning it wasn't on my dresser where I'd left it. My dresser is right next to the door. Anyone could have reached in and taken it. Well, all I can say is, if you girls are helping that man who calls himself your cousin Clyde, you'll regret it. Without your uncle's will, none of the rest of us have any legal claim to this property."

"Is that all you think of?" asked Holly. "Uncle David was right when he wrote that song. We all do want too much. I did, too, but I've changed my mind. You can leave me out of this disgusting scramble for Uncle David's property. Doesn't anyone miss him or care how he died? It wouldn't surprise me if his spirit did come back to haunt you, the way you're all acting. At least, his son has some decent feelings."

"An act!" snorted Aunt Florence. "The Potters were never demonstrative. I was fond of my brother. Why, I practically raised him. And didn't I take that ungrateful sister of yours?"

"Did you expect gratitude for separating us?" retorted Holly. Judy couldn't help admiring her spirit even though she had lost control of her temper. "You thought Ruth would be a help to you because she was the oldest," Holly charged. "Uncle David was willing to raise all three of us together. But he was poor then and his wife had started some sort of scandal about him. I never did know what it was."

"She said he neglected the baby," Cousin Cleo informed her. "One night she came home from the movies and found Clyde in convulsions. David was walking the floor with him. It turned out that he'd slapped him—"

"To bring him out of the convulsions, no doubt," Judy interrupted. "Any father might do that. You get panicky."

A doctor's daughter, Judy knew how frightening convulsions can be. It looked to her as if David Potter had been the victim of malicious gossip. Poor man! No wonder he had become so reserved.

"So now you're defending him, too! I can't understand the change in you, Doris," declared Cousin Cleo.

"You weren't particularly fond of your uncle when you were a little girl. In fact, you were afraid of him. You begged to be allowed to go to Hollywood with your cousin Arlene—"

"I didn't know what Hollywood was like then," Judy broke in before she could pursue this subject further.

Aunt Florence looked at Judy sharply.

"What happened next?" Holly asked quickly. "I mean about Cousin Clyde when he was a baby?"

"His mother managed to bring him around all right. But she would have no more to do with a man who would slap a helpless baby, and I don't blame her," Cousin Cleo declared.

"The very next day, she packed up and took the baby back to his grandmother in Florida," Aunt Florence took up the story. "David wouldn't talk about it after that, so, naturally, we felt he must have been cruel to the child and wouldn't give you girls a proper home either. Can't you see that, Holly?"

"No," Holly returned stubbornly. "I can't see it. Come on, Doris," she said to Judy. "Let's go out in the air and take a walk."

Seizing Judy's hand, she pulled her toward the door.

"We can order those groceries for you, if you want us to," Judy offered more politely. "We'll be going into town."

Aunt Florence gave her the list of needed supplies and a ten-dollar bill to pay for them.

"You can bring me back the change," she was beginning, but the black look on Holly's face stopped her. Ten dollars was hardly enough to pay for the groceries, and she had meat on the list besides.

"Whew!" Judy exclaimed when the two girls were outside in the fresh air. "They say you can pick your friends but not your relatives. My house will seem like a sanctuary after that. Let's take the path through the woods this time, so we won't be seen cutting across the pasture."

"We won't stay there long, will we?" Holly asked anxiously.

"Only long enough to try out an experiment I have in mind. Then we'll get out the car and drive on to Farringdon. I'm eager to hear what my brother has to say about this," Judy declared. "As I told you, he knew ahead of time that some house around here was going to be 'haunted,' and I intend to find out how he knew."

CHAPTER XIII

Judy's Experiment

"Wait here!" Judy directed Holly when they had come to the end of the path. "I'll run around and open the house. Then, when I signal, start walking toward the back door."

"What sort of signal will you give?" Holly asked, looking mystified.

"I'll whistle through my fingers—like this!"

It was a trick Judy had learned from her father when she was a little girl. Holly gave a start. The whistle sounded like a train.

"I'll do it," she agreed, "but I'm sure I don't understand why you want me to go in a different way. I don't really mind walking through the garden and going in the front door with you. There's nothing there now to frighten us."

The garden did seem peaceful. Judy stopped to pull a weed or two as she walked through it. There weren't many. She had taken great care of her flowers, and now their brilliance in the morning sunshine almost dazzled her.

"If I were a wandering spirit," she thought whimsically, "this garden is where I'd come, especially in the late summer when it's so beautiful."

She didn't really believe in ghosts, though it was fun to pretend she did. And, if this experiment she was about to try worked out, she'd soon have proof of what had really taken place in her garden.

"I hope I'm right. If I can explain things logically to Horace—"

Judy's thoughts were interrupted by something soft and warm brushing against her ankles. She laughed softly when she saw what it was.

"Blackberry!" she exclaimed. "You good cat to be here waiting for me."

She always talked to him as if he were a person. Taking the cat in her arms, she unlocked the front door and carried him into the house. Still holding him, she went directly to the chair by the typewriter and seated herself in the bay window.

"Keep your eyes open, Blackberry," she whispered into his fur. "We'll just see if I've figured this out."

This was the exact spot where she had been sitting when she saw the transparent purple figure. Holly had been sitting at the typewriter when they both saw the second apparition. Now to see what had caused them!

Eyes glued to the window that looked out on the garden, Judy gave a shrill whistle.

Nothing happened!

A moment more and she could hear Holly tapping gently on the back door. Judy unbolted it and let her in while Blackberry gazed solemnly from one of them to the other. Even the cat seemed puzzled.

"Tell me what this is all about," begged Holly. "I'm curious."

"It was just an experiment that didn't work," replied Judy. "I thought I'd figured out something. I thought that if there were two people who looked like your Uncle David and my grandmother, or who disguised themselves to look like them, they might have tricked us, somehow, into believing we saw what actually were only reflections. Reflections can be transparent, but there was no reflection in the window when you walked by, so that can't be the answer. Besides, who would want to trick us?"

"We may find out when we talk to your brother," Holly said hopefully. "Anyway, I'm eager to meet him."

"You will very shortly."

Judy whisked through the house, doing a few necessary chores, and then put out the cat, who was purring so loudly it sounded like a motor inside him. The purring stopped abruptly.

"He knows I'm going to leave him alone again. I don't like to do it," Judy declared. "Poor cat! This is no way to treat him."

"I envy him," declared Holly. "If you left me alone I wouldn't have a peaceful house and garden to enjoy. I'd be in a nest of greedy relatives. How I hate them!"

"Hate is a strong word," Judy chided her. "You may find some good in them yet. I don't really believe they meant to be unkind to your uncle. They just misunderstood him. It is hard to forgive them for being so greedy—"

"Or for being so unfair to Cousin Clyde," Holly put in. "He's the only one of them with any real manners. If I could be near you, Judy, I wouldn't mind so much if the property did go to him. Just think! All these years he's been without his real father and then, just when he did meet him and they were finally getting to know each other, that horrible accident had to happen. It almost seems as if fate were against him, doesn't it? Or don't you believe in fate?"

"I don't know what to believe," Judy replied honestly. "I've got to do a lot more thinking about this before I come to any conclusions. And I've got to see Horace."

Backing the car out of the garage, she and Holly were soon on their way. It was a pleasant drive over the hill that Judy used to call the top of the world and down into the valley beyond. Every stretch of woodland, every farm they passed was familiar to Judy. She had been over this road so often. But to Holly it was all strange. Vaguely she remembered this or that building from her early childhood. It was odd, Judy thought, that she remembered her uncle so well.

"Where did you last see him?" Judy asked.

"Who? Uncle David? Why, in your garden—"

"I mean before that. You may have forgotten him a little—"

"Never!" declared Holly. "Cousin Cleo brought me back for a visit just a month or so before the big flood. I remember it so well that I—why, I can even tell you what Uncle David was wearing when I last saw him sitting on the stool in front of the organ. It was a plaid shirt and corduroy pants. I remember just how his feet moved on the pedals."

"It's an old-fashioned pedal organ then? I wondered."

"Yes, and it has brackets at the sides for candles, and a lot of scrollwork. I remember it so well! I like organ music better than anything else," declared Holly. "Oh, I know it was spooky the other night, but sometimes you like to be in a sort of wondering mood. I do, especially, when I write things."

"Some day you will have to show me some of the things you've written. You've saved them, I hope."

"No, I haven't," Holly admitted. "If they weren't any good, I tore them up. And if they were, I always sent them to Uncle David. He was the only one who

ever read them. I wouldn't have dared show them to
the girls at boarding school. They would have laughed
at me."

"But your uncle understood, is that it?"

"Yes, he didn't always praise them, but his criti-
cism was good. He promised me that if I ever wrote
anything good enough, he'd set it to music. So I tried
verse. And there were scads of stories. I'm sure Uncle
David saved them. They'll be thrown out if the relatives find them, I'm afraid. Oh, I hope they don't. I
hope Uncle David has them all safe in that locked
room. I hope he has his music there, too. And if he did
make a will I'm sure that must be where he put it.
You know, Judy, it could be that Cousin Fred is trying to protect Uncle David's things. I mean, if Cousin
Fred is the one who is playing ghost. I don't really
think he can play the organ, though. Cousin Cleo
would certainly know of it. Oh, Judy!" Holly broke
off as they crossed a bridge and came into town,
"we're there, aren't we? I do remember the big courthouse clock."

"Yes," Judy replied. "This is Farringdon. Now, if
I can find a place to park—"

"There! That car's just pulling out."

Judy quickly maneuvered her car into the vacated
space. When she had parked it, she and Holly got out
and crossed the street.

"That's the office of the Farringdon *Daily Herald*

right opposite the courthouse," she pointed out as the two girls hurried toward it.

The big clock struck twelve.

"Perfect timing!" Judy exclaimed. "Horace will just be going out for lunch. Hurry, Holly! I think I see him now."

CHAPTER XIV

A Weird Communication

HORACE BOLTON, star reporter for the Farringdon *Daily Herald*, was heading for the nearest restaurant. He was alone and seemed to be concentrating on one thought—food.

"Horace!" Judy called.

She had to call her brother once more before he turned around.

"Sis!" he exclaimed in surprise. "For Pete's sake, what are you doing here in Farringdon?"

Judy laughed.

"It isn't for Pete's sake. Peter is away, as you very well know. It's for Holly's sake. Horace, I want to introduce you to a new friend of mine, Holly Potter."

Horace studied Holly a moment, apparently liking what he saw. Then he beamed and held out his hand.

111

"Holly Potter! You're not a new friend," he declared. "Where have you been all these years? Why, I remember you as a little tot about so high." And he indicated a place on a level with his knee. "You are David Potter's niece, aren't you?"

"Yes. His youngest." Holly was suddenly blushing. It made her look prettier than she was. Judy could tell she was feeling shy.

If Horace noticed it he was kind enough to give no indication. Later Judy told him he sounded as if someone had wound him up. He didn't stop talking until they were seated at a table in a somewhat nicer restaurant than the one for which he had originally headed.

He ended his discourse about nothing by saying, as he took up the menu to study it, "And what brings you here, my fair sister with your equally fair companion?"

"I'm dark," Holly said abruptly. "And I'm not pretty like Judy, either."

Horace whistled.

"Who told you that?"

"My mirror."

"Well, if it tells you you're not pretty, throw it away and get a new one. No doubt your present mirror distorts your reflection."

"Speaking of reflections," Judy put in quickly, seeing an opportunity to get in a few words, "I just tried an experiment. Horace, seriously, if you saw a—a transparent person, wouldn't you think it must be a reflection of some sort?"

"If I saw a transparent person," declared Horace, "I would promptly faint dead away. I'm not the hero you undoubtedly believe me to be, my dear sister. Transparent people, as everyone knows who has ever been to the movies, are ghosts."

"Camera tricks! There must be other tricks too," Judy interrupted, refusing to be sidetracked. "But whichever it was, Holly and I both saw the transparent figure of her uncle walking in my garden."

"Her uncle? Not the one who was killed in Florida?"

Judy nodded.

"And before that I saw Grandma. Anyway, it looked like her in that purple dress she used to have. She was transparent, too."

"Great jumping grasshoppers!" exclaimed Horace. "So it wasn't a joke!"

"What wasn't?" asked Judy.

"That letter I received. It was anonymous. Such communications usually are. There's supposed to be a haunted house in the vicinity of Dry Brook Hollow. I half expected you'd find it before I did. But, honestly, Judy, I never thought the letter meant your house."

"It may not be," Judy said. " 'All houses wherein men have lived and died are haunted houses.' Remember? You quoted that poem yourself, and now Holly and I find ourselves in the peculiar position of not knowing which house is more spooky, her uncle's or mine. In mine, we see ghosts. In his, we hear them," she finished, smiling.

The waiter, who had come to take their order, overhearing part of the conversation, looked as if he wasn't quite sure he ought to serve them. But Horace's grin reassured him. While they waited, Judy told her brother about the organ music and the song, "Wanting Too Much," that had been played and sung over and over.

"It did sound like David Potter's voice," she added, "but the room where the music was coming from was locked from the inside, and still is, as far as I know."

"An old trick!" Horace commented airily. "Ghosts always prefer to enter haunted houses mysteriously through locked doors."

"It is a trick, all right, and an awfully clever one," Judy admitted. "If it isn't—well, I'm not ready to change all my theories about life and death just yet. I never believed in ghosts, and it's going to take a lot of convincing before I change my mind."

"You think someone for some reason is trying to convince you of their existence, don't you?" asked Horace.

"Yes."

"I'm just about convinced," Holly confessed.

"Well, I'm not," declared Judy. "And I still haven't given up that idea I was experimenting with. As for the music, if we hear it again tonight—"

"Judy, you are staying in that house instead of your own!" exclaimed Horace.

She smiled.

"Naturally, or didn't I tell you I'm masquerading as Holly's sister Doris?"

"Again? Don't tell me you have another double!"

Horace knew Judy had played the part of a cousin who closely resembled her not once, but several times. His sister had a way of getting involved in the most uncanny situations. And he told her so.

"I'm afraid I'm not a very good Doris," Judy admitted. "But the relatives haven't seen her for several years so they haven't found me out yet. I hate to think what will happen when they do. If I come out of this mess still using my head, as Dad always advised me to, I will deserve a medal."

"I can't give you a medal," Holly began, "but I could reward you—"

"Reward me? Haven't you done that already? You're my friend," Judy reminded her, "and a new friend is the greatest reward I can think of."

"And the least expensive," Horace added as their plates were set before them. "Oh, I don't mean the lunch," he explained to the still worried waiter.

"My brother has a habit of taking over my friends,

so watch out, Holly!" warned Judy when the waiter had retreated to a more comfortable distance. "Remember, Horace, Holly is only fifteen."

"I don't mind. Honey's turned me down for that handsome scoundrel, Forrest Dean. So I may as well start all over again."

With that threat, Horace began to eat. It was a pleasure to watch him. Judy enjoyed the lunch, too, but Holly kept looking across the table at Horace as if she wanted to ask him something but didn't quite dare. She wasn't used to boys and didn't know how to take Horace's teasing.

"Did that mysterious letter you received advise you not to divulge its contents?" Judy asked Horace.

"Oh, not at all," he replied, taking an envelope from his pocket and unfolding the piece of paper he had been carrying around in it. "As luck would have it, I have the letter with me. Lend an ear while I read you what it did advise:

" *'If you are as clever a reporter as you are said to be, you will soon have a front-page story on a haunted house in the vicinity of Dry Brook Hollow. You and that smart sister of yours had better keep your eyes and ears open. This is one time the ghost will not fail the watchers. Please be on hand'* —But it doesn't say where," Horace observed, pausing to study the letter.

"Maybe that was for us to find out," Judy speculated.

"Well, it looks as if we've done it. Or should I say you've done it? You've stolen the march on me again, sis, and I may as well admit I don't like it. Why couldn't I have been the one to see that transparent figure in the garden?"

"You said you'd faint."

"I probably would, too," Horace confessed. "Seriously, sis, are you sure you didn't make this up? A transparent form gliding through a garden in the daytime—you did say it was the daytime, didn't you?"

"Four o'clock in the afternoon, to be exact."

"Well, whenever it was, it's too fantastic for me to believe until I've seen it myself. Do I have your permission to watch this afternoon at four o'clock and see if it appears again?"

"Under one condition," said Judy. "I'll give you the keys to my house and tell you exactly where to look for the ghost, if you'll let me examine that letter you were just reading."

"May I examine it, too, Horace?" asked Holly. "I've been wanting to ask you."

"So that's what it was," Judy smiled at her. "I knew you wanted to say something, but we haven't given you much of a chance. I really think," Judy finished as Horace handed her the letter, "that Holly ought to examine this before I do. She may have some idea who wrote it."

CHAPTER XV

Startling Developments

"I DO!" Holly exclaimed. "Oh, Judy, it *is!* I was
afraid it would be."

"It is what?" asked Judy, taking the letter from
Holly's trembling hand.

"It is Uncle David's handwriting. But look at the
postmark on the envelope! Two days *after* he was
killed."

"Well, his spirit didn't write it. That's certain," declared Horace. "It's probably a plain case of forgery.
Now tell me more about these relatives who are oc-
cupying your uncle's house and why they're there."

Forgetting her shyness, Holly told him everything
at length. Then she studied the communication again.

"I have some of Uncle David's letters. Judy kept

them for me in her secret drawer. We could compare them."

"An excellent idea! I'm afraid we couldn't make a very good job of it, though," Horace added, turning to Judy. "It would take a handwriting expert. Why don't you shoot this letter and a sample of David Potter's genuine handwriting off to Peter? He will know what to do about it. Jeepers! I meant to tell you before that Peter called up Mom this morning. He thought you were staying with us when nobody answered the telephone at your house."

"What did Mother tell him?"

Horace shrugged his shoulders. "She didn't know what to tell him. She called me and said Peter left a number for you to call before one o'clock. You still have time."

"Good!"

Judy excused himself to make the call. When she returned to the table half an hour later, her luncheon plate had been cleared away and her dessert was waiting for her. Horace and Holly had finished theirs.

"What took you so long?" they asked.

"It didn't seem long," replied Judy. "I had so much to tell Peter. He says he's sure this is a trick. Someone is trying to frighten the relatives away, he thinks. I had to describe each one of them in detail and answer a million questions. Now he's worried about me and says he's coming home as soon as he can, to make sure nothing happens to me. I feel awfully guilty about it. I almost wish I hadn't told him. His own work was important, I know."

"Why didn't you tell him I'd look after you?" asked Horace.

"I did. Maybe that was what worried him," Judy giggled. "I told him you were going to watch for the ghost."

"Didn't he approve?"

"He didn't say he didn't," was the vague reply.

"Judy tried one experiment and it didn't work," Holly put in. "Now you can see if you're a better medium than she is. That is what they call people who make spirits appear, isn't it?"

"They do it in darkened rooms," Judy informed her. "Not in the bright sunshine."

They talked for a while, solving nothing. Then Horace glanced out the window of the restaurant at the courthouse clock and remembered he had a job.

"I'll visit your house on the newspaper's time," he decided. "If anything comes of it, I'll be rewarded. That is, if I survive the shock of seeing a genuine ghost."

"You've been forewarned. I think you'll survive. If nothing appears," Judy added, "it may be because the 'ghost' has removed himself to different quarters. My guess is that he may be concealed in the locked room."

"You didn't tell me where it is," Horace reminded her.

"I will," Judy promised. "One thing at a time. If the ghost in the garden doesn't materialize, then watch outside the Potter house tonight and see what happens. But remember I'm Doris," she added as they left the restaurant. "I can't invite you in."

"Your brother is fun," Holly declared when she and Judy were driving into Dry Brook Hollow with the groceries they had almost forgotten to purchase before leaving Farringdon.

"He is, isn't he? I'm glad you liked him. The next car to drive down this road will be his, I suppose. It's three o'clock now. He should be here in another hour, but we won't wait," Judy decided. "Now comes the problem of putting the car away and getting these groceries back to your uncle's house."

Holly laughed.

"Aunt Flo was really funny," she said. "She'll be sure we've run off with her ten dollars if we don't hurry. Do you think she's getting suspicious?"

"Of me? I shouldn't wonder," Judy replied, lifting the big bag of groceries out of the car.

"I'll carry the potatoes," Holly offered. "We're going to take the shortcut through the woods, aren't we? It seemed shorter, and this stuff is heavy."

It grew no lighter as the girls hurried along the seldom-used path that entered the woods just back of Judy's house and emerged not far from the Potter house on the other side of the hill.

Halfway there, Holly stopped short and gave a

little gasp. The bag of potatoes she had been carrying slid to the ground. It split open as it hit a tree root, and potatoes rolled everywhere. When Holly made no attempt to pick them up, Judy began to do it, making room for them in her bag.

"Come on, Holly, help me," she said almost impatiently.

Holly stood rooted to the path. She did not answer. Judy looked up and saw her face and was instantly sorry for her hasty words.

"What's the matter?" she asked. "Oh, Holly! You're so white. What happened? Did something frighten you?"

"It was Uncle David!" Holly whispered. "I saw him back there in the woods. I'm sure I did. But now he's gone. Do you think I imagined it?"

"I don't know, Holly. I didn't see anything."

"I did." Holly's eyes still had that wide, frightened look. "I can't stand it," she said. "I don't want to go through the rest of my life seeing ghosts."

"You won't have to," Judy said quietly. "If you saw your uncle, then maybe Horace will, too. If, some way, we can prove it's a real person masquerading as David Potter and trying to frighten us—"

"Who would be so cruel?"

"I don't know. But I intend to find out," Judy promised grimly. "This trick has gone far enough."

She spent a little time looking about for footprints,

but found none. Holly did nothing. This latest appearance, fleeting though it had been, seemed to have unnerved her completely.

"I can't bear it," she kept saying as they continued on their way along the path. "If that organ music comes again tonight, I'll scream. I know I will. I'll open my mouth and let out one scream after another until it stops."

"I wouldn't do that if I were you," Judy advised her. "Just leave it to me. We'll soon find out what sort of trickery this is. Look, Holly!"

They were approaching the Potter house. Judy stopped to scrutinize it carefully. She observed that the windows to the locked room were tightly closed and shuttered. All the other shutters were wide open. The sun shining on the windows made them appear golden. It did not look at all like a haunted house.

Judy entered through the back door and put down the groceries on the kitchen table. Holly followed close behind her. Hearing voices in the living room, they paused to listen. Aunt Flo, apparently, had not heard them come in. She was so excited that her voice actually quavered.

"Hide it, Diana! Quick, before Clyde comes in," Judy heard her whisper.

"Where?" her daughter asked breathlessly.

"Anywhere, but be quick about it! He's apt to destroy it if he finds it."

"Shall I put it back inside the clock where I found it?" Diana asked.

"Go ahead! There isn't time to look for a safer hiding place now. Here they come!" Aunt Flo exclaimed as a car stopped in front of the house.

Before Judy and Holly could decide what the two in the living room were hiding, in strode Cousin Fred and Clyde. Both were carrying groceries.

Clyde looked at the supplies Judy and Holly had brought in, and laughed.

"Everybody seems to have had the same idea. Now we have plenty of food. Who is going to cook it?"

Judy was about to volunteer when Cousin Cleo came in with still another bag of groceries and took charge of everything. She didn't want anyone to help.

"People just get in her way. I've heard that plenty of times when I've wanted to help her. Cousin Cleo is a perfectionist," Holly explained. "Her house is so clean it makes anyone uncomfortable to live in it. This will be a perfect dinner, too. Just wait and see if it isn't."

Holly was right. The dinner turned out to be a great success. Everyone complimented Cousin Cleo on her skill as a cook. She beamed at the other relatives, who were all being extremely pleasant to each other tonight. Diana's smile reminded Judy of the cat who has just eaten the canary. Her mother went so far as to compliment Judy and Holly on the manner in which they had spent her ten dollars.

"You spent it wisely. This food is delicious," she said.

"We aren't responsible for the roast. We bought chopped meat and a pound of bacon," Judy began.

"How nice!" Aunt Florence murmured. "They will do for breakfast and lunch tomorrow. Mmm! Delicious!" she approved as the dessert was brought in.

Cousin Cleo had made Dutch apple cake and topped it with whipped cream. All the relatives exclaimed over it as they ate. It amused Judy just to listen to them. Secretly, she knew, each was plotting to get David Potter's property away from the other.

Cousin Fred, usually so morose, was the most amiable of all. Dinner was hardly over when he offered to treat anyone who cared to go with him to a movie in Roulsville.

"Is it a mystery?" his wife asked.

"No, a romance."

"Then I'll go," Cousin Cleo decided. "I wouldn't want to see a mystery after what happened in this house last night. A romance is different. How about you, Clyde? Are you going with us?"

"I'm going, too!" cried Diana when her handsome young cousin had accepted the invitation.

"How about you two girls?"

Holly opened her mouth to speak, but Judy was too quick for her.

"No, thank you," she said. "Holly and I would rather stay here. The ghost might not like it if we all went away," she added, smiling. "Do you think so, Holly?"

"Definitely not," she said, but her eyes were puzzled. When the others were gone, she turned to Judy and asked, "What was the idea? I would have enjoyed seeing that movie."

"More than you would enjoy seeing your uncle's will?" Judy questioned. "I'm sure that must be what Diana was hiding in the clock."

CHAPTER XVI

The Hiding Place

"It isn't here!" declared Holly, turning away from the mantel in disappointment. "There's nothing inside the clock except the key Diana must have been using to wind it when she made the discovery. They've probably hidden the will somewhere else."

Judge felt all around inside the clock to make sure. But Holly was right. Judy's fingers touched nothing except the key and the pendulum, which had stopped. She started it swinging again before she closed the glass door of the clock.

"I succeeded in stopping it," she admitted, "but I didn't find anything either. Maybe it wasn't the will they were hiding. We have no proof that it was."

"They said Cousin Clyde might destroy it. What

else would they be afraid he might destroy?" asked Holly.

Judy shrugged her shoulders.

"Who knows? Aunt Florence has been suspicious of him from the first, calling him an impostor and all."

"I don't believe he'd destroy the will, anyway," declared Holly. "He seems honest and I like him. It makes me just sick to see how sweet they all are to him to his face and then how they turn right around and suspect him of all sorts of things behind his back. Don't you hate it, Judy?"

"I do hate insincerity," Judy replied, "but remember, I'm playing a part myself. We all are, even you."

"What do you mean?" asked Holly.

Judy laughed at her confusion.

"Oh, I suspect you're fonder of your relatives than you want me to think. I caught you looking at Aunt Florence almost wistfully at dinner tonight. You weren't thinking about the will then. You were wishing she cared more about you. I could tell."

"You're a mind reader, aren't you? I would like to like her," confessed Holly. "Maybe it's because she reminds me of Uncle David. She is his sister and I do believe she was fond of him, but, as she says, the Potters aren't demonstrative. I wish they were. I'd like to be the sort of girl who folds up and weeps when things go wrong. It would be easier."

"Would it?" asked Judy. "I cry occasionally, but

it never solves anything. It only gives me a headache."
She paused, setting down the pile of dishes she had
been carrying. She and Holly had started clearing the
table.

"What's the matter?" asked Holly. "You look as if
an idea had hit you right between the eyes."

"It has. Speaking of solving things, this is just the
opportunity we've been waiting for," Judy announced. "We may be able to solve the mystery of the
organ music we heard last night. There must be another door to the locked room, and I intend to find it.
Come on, Holly, let's explore the upstairs rooms."

"You do it while I start the dishes," Holly said.
"We don't want the relatives to come back and find
them here on the sink. Anyway, I like washing
dishes."

She called this last astonishing statement from the
kitchen, where she was already running hot water.

"I'll dry them later," Judy promised.

"There's plenty of time," Holly assured her. "You
don't mind going up alone, do you? If anything happens, just yell."

"What could happen?" asked Judy as she started
up the stairs.

At the top she paused to listen for a moment. No
sound came from either Aunt Florence's bedroom,
which was just opposite the stairway, or the one beyond it. Judy had not watched the relatives leave for

the movies, but she felt sure they had all gone, as none of them seemed to be anywhere about.

Tiptoeing down the hall to the mysterious room, Judy tried the door. It was still locked from the inside.

"There must be some other entrance," she thought. "There has to be."

Glancing back to make sure no one else had come up the stairs behind her, she moved to the door of the room occupied by Cousin Cleo and her husband, who might, just possibly, be the mysterious musician.

The door was tightly closed.

"Have I any right to open it?" Judy asked herself.

The answer, she felt, was that she did have the right. Peter wouldn't hesitate about entering another person's room if he felt it to be necessary to the solution of one of his cases. Why should she?

Her mind made up, Judy turned the knob. To her delight, the door opened. She entered the room quickly and looked around. Everything was in apple pie order. The twin beds were made. Cousin Cleo's flowered housecoat lay across a chair arm, but her other things were neatly put away either in the closet or in the large dresser that stood against the opposite wall.

"That's the wall where the door would have to be," thought Judy.

She had seen at first glance that there was no ordinary door connecting the two rooms, but the idea of a door—possibly a hidden one—still persisted in her mind. She peered behind the dresser. Then she moved it and placed her hands flat against the wall behind it.

"I was wrong," she whispered. "It's solid plaster."

She did not search the closet. There was no need of it as the closet door opened from the opposite side of the room. But she did fling open the window and lean out as far as she dared to inspect the outside of the house.

"The shutters are locked just as I thought they were. It would be impossible to climb in through the windows, even with a ladder," Judy decided.

The room was a fortress, as far as she could see. Disappointed again, Judy returned to the hall just in time to hear a door close quietly. Had someone seen her leaving the room she had been so reluctant to enter? Who was there to see her? Holly was still rattling dishes downstairs, and all the other relatives had gone. She thought it was the door to Aunt Florence's room that had opened, but she couldn't be sure.

"Maybe it was my imagination playing tricks on me again," she whispered.

Once more she tiptoed to the door at the end of the hall. Was this the door that had closed so quietly? As Judy stood tensely listening she thought she heard soft footsteps behind it.

"Is it our friend the ghost?" she wondered aloud.

Someone chuckled! It was an amused chuckle, but it made Judy shiver. She shook the door and called, "Who's there?" but there was no answer, only a little click and a noise as of something sliding. Again Judy shivered.

Crouching beside the door, she waited to see what would happen next. Was that click a signal for the organ to start playing? Judy listened for the first strains of the mysterious music, but heard nothing. Should she go downstairs and tell Holly?

At that precise moment, Holly called from the kitchen.

"Judy! What's taking you so long? The dishes are all washed. Now I'm drying them."

"I'll be right down to help you," Judy called back.

Her voice echoed strangely. Or was that an echo? Never superstitious, Judy did not believe this house was really haunted. Nor her own house either. If she could only explain that transparent form of her grandmother floating about in her garden. Was it just a strong feeling, as the poem suggested? Or had she really seen it?

"Well, we both saw the transparent figure of David Potter," she told herself. "I wonder what he was like when Holly saw him this afternoon in the woods."

Deciding to ask her, Judy tiptoed along the hall until she reached the stairway. There she paused, listening again. Had she been mistaken about the footsteps? Now she seemed to hear them behind the door of the room occupied by Aunt Florence and her daughter. That was a little more logical. The older woman might have remained at home after all. There had been no reason to enter her room, as it was too far from the room at the end of the hall for there to be any connecting door.

"Judy!" Holly called again.

Holly should have called her Doris, Judy thought. If any of the relatives were at home, they would surely be suspicious of her now.

"Coming!" she called back.

She was about to descend the stairs when a door creaked, and again she heard footsteps.

Whirling around, she saw that it was the door to Aunt Florence's room that had opened. Cousin Cleo, of all people, stood there, her eyes gleaming triumphantly.

CHAPTER XVII

On the Verge of Discovery

"You!" exclaimed Judy, staring in disbelief.
"Cousin Cleo, you aren't—you can't be—"

"No, I'm not a ghost, if that's what you're trying
to say."

Judy had been stammering in her excitement.

"But you're here when I thought you had gone to
the movies," she protested.

"That was exactly what I wanted you to think,"
declared Cousin Cleo. "I was curious to see just what
you two girls would do if you were left alone in the
house." Pausing for emphasis, she glared at Judy and
added, "Now I know!"

"What do you know?" asked Judy.

She didn't mean to be rude. She was really curious.

Had she heard Holly call her Judy instead of Doris? Cousin Cleo didn't tell her. She merely looked daggers at her and said, "I know plenty. Make no mistake about that. I've suspected all along that you were up to something, and you aren't the only one. I wouldn't advise you to do any more exploring if you know what's good for you, especially in other people's rooms."

"That is good advice," agreed Judy, "but weren't you exploring a little bit yourself? Just what were you doing in Aunt Florence's room?"

"What have all of us been doing ever since we came here?" she retorted. "Looking for David Potter's will, though I fail to see what you expect to get out of this, if your name is Judy. The real Doris will show up before long and then where will you be?"

"I've thought of that," Judy admitted, deciding that the truth was best, after all. "As for what I expect to get out of it, I may as well tell you that I expect to get nothing at all except the satisfaction of helping someone I like out of a pretty desperate situation."

"You won't get any thanks for it. I didn't," Cousin Cleo snapped.

Hearing their voices, Holly hurried up the stairs and faced her cousin.

"What's the matter?" she asked. "Why are you looking at—at Doris as if she'd committed a crime? She isn't to blame for any of the spooky things that have been going on around here, and I think you know it. If anybody is trying to haunt this house, it's Cousin Fred."

"Oh, Holly! You shouldn't have said that," Judy protested. "We can't be sure until we find that other door."

"What other door?" demanded Cousin Cleo. "Where is it?"

"I wish I knew," replied Judy. "I was looking for it myself when I took the liberty of entering your room. I'm really sorry, but I had to do it. We can't go through another night like last night. There must be some other way of getting into that room at the end of the hall where the music was playing. The door is locked from the inside."

"I noticed that the day we came here," Cousin Cleo admitted in a more friendly tone. "I'd like to find that other door myself, if there is one, and so would Fred. But there's no way of getting in there from our room, as you probably found out. Fred and I went over every inch of the wall before you came. There's nothing under the wallpaper but solid plaster. I'm convinced of it."

Judy was convinced of it, too, but Holly had to be shown. It occurred to Judy that she might have asked and been admitted to the room herself. Cousin Cleo seemed willing enough to let Holly explore.

"Did you look behind this dresser, Doris?" she asked.

Judy nodded.

"I'm afraid it's a little late to be calling me Doris," she added. "Cousin Cleo knows who I am."

"She does!"

Explanations were in order, and Holly made them.

"It was my idea," she admitted. "I asked Judy to be Doris. I needed someone."

Cousin Cleo did not dispute that. She even acted a little embarrassed. Probably she had sensed Holly's need herself, but her naturally cold disposition had not allowed her to unbend. And Holly still suspected her husband.

"Where was Cousin Fred last night when the music was playing?" she asked abruptly as they left the room and paused beside the door at the end of the hall.

"Sleeping. He's lucky. I haven't had a good night's rest since we came here," Cousin Cleo complained. "You should have seen the condition of this house. Dust and cobwebs over everything. I'm surprised your uncle could live in it the way it was. I got here first and put it to rights—all except this room," she added, shaking the doorknob. "He must have put something awfully private in there if there is a secret entrance."

"Maybe that's where he put his will," Judy suggested, watching Cousin Cleo's face.

She might have overheard the conversation in the living room, too. She could have been the one to re-move the will that Judy felt certain Diana must have hidden in the clock. Her next words, however, convinced Judy that she had overheard nothing.

"I'm sure it is!" she declared. "I've searched everywhere else. If that will doesn't turn up before long, I'm going to break this door down and go in there and look around for it myself."

Saying this, she shook the door to the locked room so violently that the key fell out of the lock. Judy heard a little *ping!* as it hit the floor.

Holly, apparently, did not hear it. Neither did Cousin Cleo. They were busy talking. Judy paid very little attention to what they were saying. Her mind was on one thing. That key! If she could find some way to catch hold of it she knew she could slide it underneath the door. There was a wide crack. What she couldn't understand was why no light came through it when the organ was playing. Or had the mysterious organist been playing and singing in the dark?

Judy shivered at this thought. Holly was telling Cousin Cleo about the apparition she had seen in the woods that afternoon, but Judy refused to believe that a transparent phantom had actually entered the room through the locked door.

"I'll soon have the door open," she thought. "Then I'll see what it was."

Making some excuse, she went up to the room she and Holly shared in the attic. Only one portion of the attic was finished. The rest was used for storage. Things had been thrown about carelessly. Apparently the search for the lost will had included this storage room in the attic. Only the tools and other miscellaneous hardware in the drawer of a workbench under the window were undisturbed.

Judy picked up a long screw driver, looked at it speculatively and put it back. No, that wouldn't do it. She'd need some sort of a hook to catch hold of the key.

"I hope it didn't fall too far away from the door," she thought, still searching.

At last she found the perfect tool for her purpose.

"A magnet!" she whispered, almost pouncing upon the desired object.

It was a small, flat horseshoe magnet. First Judy tried it out on a few nails to make sure it was powerful enough to attract the key. It was!

"Good!" she exulted to herself. "I'll attach a string to it, or better yet, a piece of this wire."

When the wire she had found was securely attached to the magnet, Judy concealed the strange tool behind her back and tiptoed down to the second floor. Holly and her cousin had gone down to the kitchen. Judy's heart was beating wildly. She couldn't help feeling that she was on the verge of making a great discovery and could hardly wait to see what lay behind the mysterious locked door.

Down on her hands and knees, Judy slid the magnet easily under the door. Manipulating the wire, she moved it about until, at last, it came in contact with something hard and metallic.

"The key!" she thought. "Now, at last, I have it!"

Her hands trembled with excitement as she withdrew it and inserted it in the lock. She was so absorbed in her task that she did not hear the relatives returning from the movies until the stairs creaked behind her and a voice asked curiously, "Is that you, Doris? What are you doing?"

It was Diana, Judy saw when she turned around. She tried not to act surprised. Dropping the key in her pocket, she gave a quick backward kick and the magnet, wire and all, disappeared under the door.

"I'll open it later," she thought. Aloud she said, "Oh, I was just wondering, but I guess it's still locked. Did you want me for something?"

"I certainly did," replied Diana. "Everybody is supposed to assemble in the living room downstairs. Mamma sent me up here to tell you. She and I have a little surprise."

"A surprise?" Judy questioned.

She might have had a little surprise of her own if Diana hadn't discovered her in the very act of opening the locked door. Had she seen the key? Judy thought not. She could feel the weight of it in her pocket as they descended the stairs together.

In the living room they found Clyde kneeling before the fireplace kindling a fire with wad after wad
of crumpled paper. Something about his actions made
Judy momentarily suspicious.

"What are you burning?" she demanded.

CHAPTER XVIII

A Piece of Burned Paper

As CLYDE POTTER whirled around to answer her question, Judy noticed that he had also placed some kindling wood and a back log in the fireplace.

"What is that paper you're burning?" she repeated, her suspicions somewhat allayed.

"Just some old newspapers I found in the cellar," he replied, smiling in his convincing way. "I thought it would do to start a fire. The house seemed a little chilly. The others will be coming in soon. Aunt Florence has promised us a surprise."

"So Diana was telling me."

"I have no idea what it is," he continued, "but I'm willing to provide the warmth for our family reunion.

142

Here they come now," he observed as the room began to fill up with relatives.

"How nice!" Aunt Florence exclaimed, walking over to the fireplace. "It's really quite warm outdoors, but this fire does make it cozy inside. Is everybody here?"

Cousin Fred was the last to come in. Holly found a place on the sofa beside Judy and whispered, "I haven't the faintest idea what this is all about, have you?"

"Not the faintest, unless—"

She stopped. Aunt Florence was looking at her as if she had spoken aloud in church.

"If you two girls have finished whispering," she said, "I have something of importance to announce. As you all know, there's a locked room upstairs. Well, I've come to the conclusion that my brother, David Potter, locked it himself to protect his valuables against intruders."

She looked at Clyde as she said this. Then her gaze shifted back to Judy and Holly.

"You two girls were trying to get in there, I know. Diana told me, but it will do you no good. The door is locked from the inside. And if you stayed home from the movies because you hoped you might find your uncle's will somewhere in the house, I may as well tell you that it has already been found."

"It has!"

The news came more as a shock than a surprise to some of the relatives, Judy suspected. She glanced at Clyde to see how he was taking it, but his expression told her nothing. Nobody spoke for a minute. Then Diana, forgetting her usual shyness, walked over toward the fireplace. The clock, so like the one Judy's grandmother had left her, stood on the mantel above it. Diana paused dramatically before opening the decorated glass door. As she felt around inside the clock her face became puzzled, then frightened.

"Mamma!" she screamed. "Someone has taken it!"

Although Judy regretted it almost instantly, her first impulse was to laugh. Diana sounded exactly like a spoiled child running to its mother and crying because someone has stolen its lollypop. But when Aunt Florence turned to accuse Judy of the theft, it ceased to be so funny.

"You found the will and destroyed it," she charged. "That was why you stayed home from the movies! Cleo won't admit it, but she's suspected all along that you weren't the real Doris Potter, and now I'm beginning to think she was right. You're another impostor like this smooth-talking young man who calls himself your cousin—"

"Who *is* her cousin," Clyde interrupted quietly.

Cousin Cleo smiled knowingly at Judy but, surprisingly enough, said nothing.

"Did I really convince her that I was doing this for Holly's good?" Judy wondered.

Apparently, Cousin Cleo was on her side, but not Aunt Flo. She continued hurling accusations at Judy until Clyde came to her rescue.

"You have no proof that anything you're saying against Doris is true," he reminded her. "As for this will you say she destroyed, I don't believe there ever was one. Naturally, my father did not anticipate his death. In fact, he told me himself that he felt he ought to get better acquainted with his relatives before making any disposition of his property."

"Indeed! So you discussed it with him? You—you vulture!"

Aunt Flo was trembling with anger. The others, excepting Diana, were inclined to agree with Clyde that there might not have been any will in the first place.

"I'm sure I never saw it," Cousin Cleo stated.

"Nor I," her husband echoed. "Clyde's argument certainly sounds reasonable to me. He's entitled to the property legally—"

"He is not!"

It angered Aunt Flo that the others should doubt her word. Judy had anticipated trouble. She glanced at the few charred remains of the paper Clyde had used to start the fire, and she knew Clyde caught her looking. Could he have deliberately burned the will?

Of all the assembled relatives, he seemed the most amiable. Judy didn't know what to think.

"I didn't actually see it, but I did hear Aunt Florence and Cousin Diana talking about a paper they had put back in the clock," she admitted. "Others might have overheard the same conversation. I'm not making any accusations, but it does look to me as if there might have been a will—"

"I don't care!" Holly burst out. "I didn't come here to grab Uncle David's property, anyway. All this squabbling makes me tired. I'm going up to bed."

"Wait a minute, Holly," Cousin Cleo stopped her. "Exactly why *did* you come here? I don't believe you've told us."

Holly stiffened.

"Not because I was invited. I wasn't!" she retorted and ran on upstairs.

Cousin Cleo gazed after her in bewilderment. Then she turned to Judy.

"I'd like to know more about this conversation you overheard," she began. "I looked in the clock myself. There was nothing at all inside it but the clock key."

"This whole thing looks like a hoax to me," declared Clyde.

"A hoax, is it? You're the hoax!" shouted Aunt Flo. "A professional house-haunter, that's what you are. You're a—a—"

"A scoundrel, Aunt Flo? Wasn't that the word you

were groping for? Perhaps I do take after my father," Clyde said amiably. "You used to call him names, too, didn't you?"

"And what if I did!"

Aunt Florence glared at her handsome young tormenter. Then she whirled upon her other nephew, Fred Potter, and remarked on the significance of his silence. This angered Cleo.

Leaving them embattled in another argument, Clyde calmly said good night and closed the two doors to the study. He was still using it as a bedroom until the locked door to the room upstairs could be opened.

"I'll have to wait to open it until things have quieted down a little," Judy decided.

The very thought of what she might discover made her tingle with excitement. She wondered if Horace had come, as he had said he might, to watch and listen outside the house.

"He heard plenty if he did," she chuckled to herself.

The quarrelsome voices of the relatives still came to her from upstairs. She was alone in the living room now, the others all having gone to their rooms.

"I wonder," she said aloud.

Then she smiled, thinking of Peter and how he used to call her his "I wonder" girl. She liked it better than "Angel," his other nickname for her. There was nothing angelic about the suspicions that were growing in her mind concerning Clyde Potter.

"I'll be ashamed of them if he's innocent," she thought.

Just to prove his innocence to her own satisfaction, Judy walked over to the fireplace and began poking about in the ashes on the hearth.

"Newspaper! It was newspaper and kindling wood, just as he said," she reproved herself.

She was about to give up her search among the ashes and follow the others upstairs when a burned scrap of what must have been a piece of ruled note-paper came to light. Judy snatched it from the embers and tried to read what was left of the writing on it.

. . . *eque* she made out, and below it the next line had begun *Flo* . . .

It was a strip from the margin of the paper that she had recovered. Whether or not it was in David Potter's handwriting she could not tell without making a comparison. The rest of what had been written was either blackened so badly as to be unreadable or else completely burned away.

". . . *eque* . . ." Judy puzzled. "It could be part of a will! . . . *eque, beque.* . . . That's it!" she decided. "The word was *bequeath* and it's seldom used except in wills. *I do give and bequeath* . . ."

But what was given and whether or not the *Flo* was the beginning of Aunt Florence's name, Judy feared she would never know. If she had only come downstairs a minute sooner she might have been able to save the precious document. Now all she had to prove that David Potter had left a will was this tiny piece of burned paper.

Judy placed it carefully in her pocket. She stood waiting until all was quiet on the second floor and then, with only her flashlight to show her the way, she crept quietly up the stairs.

At the top she stopped to listen. Not a sound came from behind any of the closed doors as Judy tiptoed past them toward the mysterious locked door at the end of the hall.

"Now," she thought. "Now—"

But once again her plan was thwarted. Just as she drew the key out of her pocket and turned it in the lock, a shrill scream echoed through the house.

CHAPTER XIX

A Shadowy Figure

FOR a moment Judy knew real terror. Deciding that this was no time to go in, she backed away from the door without even locking it. She had retreated as far as the attic stairs when Holly rushed down them, nearly falling over her.

"What happened?" she gasped. "Judy, are you all right? I had just discovered you weren't in bed beside me when I heard that scream. I thought you were being killed or something. That wasn't you scream-ing, was it?"

Judy laughed a little shakily.

"I was going to ask you the same question. You said you would scream if the organ started playing again. And it is playing! Listen!"

150

Suddenly music was swelling and throbbing all around them. At the same time, a baritone voice started singing, faintly at first, and then more distinctly.

"It is Uncle David!" cried Holly, beginning to tremble.

"Whoever it is, he knows that song well and has some reason for singing it," declared Judy. "Let's just listen for a moment . . ."

"The house of today must have each latest touch;
  No peace have the inmates; they're wanting too
      much!
  They're wanting too much that they don't really
      need.
  Their wants and their wishes cause trouble to breed.
  Says I to myself, there are many of such
  Whose trouble in life is they're wanting too much,
  Wanting too much, wanting too much—"

Judy reached up and snapped on the hall light as another scream interrupted the song.

Clyde Potter raced up the stairs, his face as white as chalk. This was no act, Judy felt sure. He could scarcely speak.

"Who—who's singing?" he managed to blurt out when he saw Judy and Holly listening at the door.

"The ghost," Judy informed him calmly. "We told

you about him but you wouldn't believe us. Now perhaps you will."

Cousin Cleo was the next one to appear in the hall.

"What's going on?" she wanted to know. "Who was that screaming?"

"It must have been Diana," Judy concluded. "The scream sounded from Aunt Florence's room. It wasn't the music that frightened her, though. She let out one scream before it began, and now listen to her!"

"Get the horrible thing out of here!" Diana was screeching. "There it is under the bed! Quick, hit it with the broom!"

"I'll do no such thing!" her mother retorted. "It won't hurt you if you stop poking at it. There it goes!"

What it was Judy could not imagine until the door burst open and the poor creature fled from the room.

"Why, it—it's Blackberry!" Holly whispered.

Judy gathered the frightened cat in her arms and began to stroke him.

"Your cat?" Cousin Cleo questioned Judy in a low voice as Clyde turned abruptly toward the stairs, muttering something about bad luck.

"Yes, he must have followed me here. But how did he get shut in Aunt Florence's room unless—"

She stopped as it suddenly came over her that Blackberry might provide the most important clue she had. Perhaps he would be bad luck for Clyde Potter, and no mistake.

Cousin Cleo must have guessed her thoughts. She jerked her head toward the stairway.

"Let Clyde think it's a stray. I can see he didn't care much for the idea of having a black cat around, but I'll see that no harm comes to your cat," she promised.

Judy was grateful and told her so.

"She sounded almost human, didn't she?" asked Holly when Cousin Cleo had returned to her room and the house was quiet once more.

"I'm beginning to like her," declared Judy. "She is cold on the surface, but underneath I don't think she is at all. She could tell I wanted Blackberry here with me. He's helped me solve mysteries before. Maybe he came on purpose to help with this one," she added, laughing.

Holly laughed too.

"Down the chimney, probably, like Santa Claus. I can't think of any other way he could get into the house. There are screens on all the windows, and we certainly didn't let him in through the outside door."

"No, but maybe someone else did." Judy was puzzled, too. "What I can't understand is how he happened to be in Aunt Florence's room. Do you think Cousin Cleo feels responsible for him because she let him in and doesn't want to say so?"

"She did act funny about it. Didn't you find out anything?"

"Not much," Judy replied, "but I hope I will."

"I hope so, too," declared Holly. "I keep thinking about that music and wondering. It was so like Uncle David's voice, though I haven't heard him sing for a long time, of course. Nobody else could sing like him except my father, and he's dead, too."

"Waldo Abson could sing a little like him," Judy said thoughtfully.

Holly's eyes widened.

"Could he be the one?"

"I've considered it," Judy admitted. "It doesn't make sense, but he is tricky. And he did laugh at us."

"We must have looked funny running through the field after we saw that—that—"

"Call it a ghost," Judy suggested. "I can't think of anything better to call it until we find out what it really was."

"Do you think we can find out?"

"I'm sure we can. Maybe before the night is over."

"Oh, Judy!" Holly said gratefully. "I'm so glad. You were investigating something in the living room, weren't you? I noticed you stayed behind when all the others left."

"Well, yes, I was," Judy admitted, not telling her anything definite.

What she had learned was certainly nothing for Holly to be glad about and telling her of it would only make matters worse. Could Clyde Potter have actually burned the will, as Judy suspected, and engineered some trick to frighten the relatives away from the house? Judy had to have proof of it before telling anyone of her suspicions. Holly didn't even know she had the key.

"You aren't going to do any more investigating tonight, are you?" she asked.

"I'd like to," replied Judy. "Now that Blackberry's here to help me I'd really be disappointed if nothing more happened. You go back to bed if you like. I'll be all right. Just switch off the light as you go by. I prefer to work in the dark."

"You're a strange girl," said Holly, "and that cat of yours is stranger still. He looks so wise you almost expect him to talk."

"He could tell us something, at that."

Holly looked at the cat speculatively. Then she said, "I don't know how you'll make out in the dark, but he should do all right. As for me, I have an annoying habit of falling asleep about this time. Don't you ever require sleep yourself?"

"Hardly ever," replied Judy, laughing.

She certainly couldn't sleep until she had had at least one glimpse of the mysteries that lay behind the door she had unlocked. Luckily, none of the relatives had tried it before when the music was playing. It had stopped with Diana's second scream, but Judy fully expected to hear it again before the night was over. Then she would see who was playing. This time she intended to let nothing stop her.

Without meaning to, Judy glanced at the door. Her voice was a little too eager as she assured Holly for the second time that she would be all right.

"I don't know about that," Holly said. "Anyway, why should you have all the fun? That door fascinates me, too. And look at Blackberry! He's planted himself in front of it just as if he expected you to open it. There! He's pricked up his ears. Do you think he hears something?"

"The music!" exclaimed Judy. "It's beginning again. Now I have to investigate!"

"How can you when the door's still locked? Or isn't it?"

Before Judy could stop her, Holly had turned the knob.

"Why, it opens!" she gasped as the door swung inward upon the shadowy room. The two girls slipped inside and closed the door quietly.

In the dim light from the hall Judy glimpsed a tall figure seated before an organ.

"He was playing in the dark! I have to see who he is!" Judy thought, turning her flashlight directly upon the face of the organist.

What she saw gave her such a start that she dropped the flashlight. Holly didn't scream. She simply slipped to the floor. It took Judy but a minute to revive her and recover the flashlight. Once more she directed its wavering beam toward the organ.

"I can't believe it!" she gasped.

The organ stool was empty. And when Judy looked around the room for Blackberry she discovered that her cat, too, had disappeared.

CHAPTER XX

The Locked Room

"It REALLY was Uncle David—or his ghost," declared Holly when she had recovered her speech. "I guess I blacked out for a minute when I saw him. What happened?"

"I wish I knew!" replied Judy. "I dropped my flashlight. Nobody went out the door. I'm sure of that. There was a sliding sound at the other end of the room, though. Let's see if we can find out what it was."

Walking across the room, Judy turned on a floor lamp that stood beside the organ. Holly followed her, still in a daze.

"I feel as if I'd been dreaming," she said, "but at least the organ is real. Uncle David did move it up

158

here just as I thought. Somehow the music doesn't seem half so frightening now that I know the organ is here."

"That isn't all that's here," commented Judy as the light she had just turned on showed her the entire room.

It was a little gloomy, like the rooms downstairs, because of the dark oak panels all around it. The ceiling and walls above the panels were covered with scenic paper suggesting a woodland bower. Judy liked it. Although the room was a little cluttered, it was tastefully furnished with a studio couch, a couple of rocking chairs and one shabby overstuffed chair with a magazine-strewn table next to it. A tall music cabinet stood beside the organ, which Judy approached a little apprehensively.

"Don't touch it," Holly warned her. "You might wake somebody—"

"It won't play if I don't touch the pedals. See!"

Holly shivered as Judy's fingers ran noiselessly along the keys.

"That's what I call ghost music," she said. "It takes real feet to pedal an organ like this and real hands to play it. Besides, Blackberry's a real cat and he disappeared, too. When we find him I suspect we'll find the answer to a lot of other questions."

"He certainly knew the way out of here," agreed Holly.

"And he didn't go out through the door," Judy added. "Well, I've discovered secret exits and entrances before, and I guess I can do it again. Usually there's something you press to open a panel—"

"Like that secret drawer you showed me!" exclaimed Holly. "Maybe it's something on the organ."

Judy eyed it speculatively.

"There's a whole row of organ stops back of the keys. I'm tempted to press them, one by one, and see what happens."

"Don't! It might start playing by itself and you know how the relatives feel about the music. They'll accuse us of being responsible for it. I'm not sure I like it in here," Holly said nervously. "Let's leave."

"Wait!" Judy stopped her. "I've discovered something. You see how dusty this music cabinet is. The top of the organ is dusty too, and there are paw marks all over it. Blackberry was in here before and spent quite a lot of time prowling around. I'm sure of it."

"He has the clue all right," agreed Holly. "I don't see any other tracks, though. I mean any human ones."

"They wouldn't show on the rug," Judy pointed out, "but look at the organ stool! Not a speck of dust on it! Someone real must have sat there. A ghost wouldn't disturb the dust."

"You talk about ghosts just as if you were well acquainted with them," Holly said.

"I am," declared Judy, "and they're all fakes. Someone has been coming in here secretly and playing the organ on purpose to frighten people—"

"Well, it's taught me a lesson," Holly interrupted. "We do want too much, every single one of us. It was horrible of me to talk the way I did about changing this house when it's just the way Uncle David wanted it. Anyway, this room is. I guess he did change the rest of it a little after the relatives began picking on him. Cousin Cleo was the worst. He wrote me about it. That's what he meant in the song when he said the house of today must have each latest touch. He meant this house! They didn't let him have any peace in it so he moved all the things he cared about up here."

"I can see that. This room is a regular storehouse." Judy opened the music cabinet. "Holly!" she exclaimed. "Just look at all the stuff in here."

"My stories!" cried Holly, taking a checked composition book from one of the shelves. "Bless Uncle David's dear old heart! He did save them. But where's all his precious music?"

"It must be here," declared Judy, "unless—"

"Unless what?" Holly asked eagerly when Judy stopped.

"Well, I was thinking that perhaps someone else borrowed it to learn it."

"You mean the—the ghost?"

"Yes, he sings like your uncle and, apparently, looks

like him. It could be a disguise, and an imitation. Naturally, the person who's playing ghost had to learn the music well in order to play it in the dark."

"I see what you mean. He must have taken it out through the secret exit—if there is one," Holly agreed. "Maybe there isn't, though. These panels are all solid and I can't find anything to press."

"I can't either," Judy admitted. "Maybe if we come back here in the daylight—"

"Can we?" asked Holly. "Do we dare leave?"

"I don't see why not. As you suggested before, we do require some sleep. My eyes are beginning to feel heavy and I'm sure my mind will be clearer in the morning."

"Yes, but Judy," Holly objected, "if the others find out the door is unlocked they'll all be in here too."

"That's easy to arrange," Judy replied with a smile as she took the key from her pocket. "We'll simply lock it again as we go out."

Holly was amazed. She had to hear all about how Judy had recovered the key.

"I intend to keep it," Judy finished, "until I find out who's been coming in here without it—and how. You see, Holly, I don't trust your relatives either, especially your cousin Clyde."

"For goodness sakes, why? He's the nicest of all. I like him the very best," declared Holly, looking at Judy with sudden resentment.

"I'm sure he meant you to."

Judy had been leafing through some of the loose papers she had found in the music cabinet. She seized upon a telegram and, after reading it, handed it to Holly.

"Here, read this," she directed. "Maybe you won't think so much of your cousin Clyde when you've finished."

The telegram read:

WILL GLADLY ATTEND REUNION BUT LACK FUNDS. SEND CHECK TO YOUR PRODIGAL SON . . .

"What does he mean by calling himself a prodigal son?" asked Holly.

"No doubt he expected his father to kill the fatted calf and put shoes on his feet and a ring on his hand, like in the Bible. Seriously," Judy said, "I think he has just one object in view—money. And no scruples about how he gets it! Your uncle must have suspected as much and so, instead of sending the check he asked for, he went down to Florida himself to check on him."

"Do you really think so?"

"I'm sure of it," Judy said. "Undoubtedly he was checking on all the relatives. Maybe that's why you and your sisters weren't invited to the reunion. He didn't need to check on you. He already knew you loved him."

"Oh, Judy! Do you think that was it? I'd feel so much better if I knew I still had his love. I never really believed in ghosts, but I do believe something lives on after people die. That's the way I feel about my father and mother. That's the reason I can bear it. I know they loved me and their love is still with me. It will always be with me—and so will Uncle David's."

Judy gave a start. She thought she heard someone cough almost at her elbow. Holly was crying softly. For the first time since she had learned of her uncle's death, she was really crying. Judy took her arm and drew her out of the room. Locking the door, Judy led her back up to the attic, where Holly soon cried herself to sleep.

"Poor kid!" Judy thought as she slipped into bed beside her. "She's really in a jam. I'm sure her uncle meant her to have this house, but now his will is burned and that 'prodigal son' of his will get everything unless—"

She was thinking of the piece of burned paper she had saved so carefully. But in the morning, when she looked between the pages of Longfellow's poems, where she had placed it for safekeeping, before going to bed, the one clue she had counted on was gone.

CHAPTER XXI

Behind the Wall

"WHAT are you doing?" asked Holly from the bed.

She had been awakened by the ruffling of the pages as Judy searched frantically for the clue she had saved. She was convinced it had been taken by someone who had entered the attic during the night, someone who must have known she had it. But it would do no good to tell Holly and alarm her. Things were bad enough for her as it was.

"Have you lost something?" Holly persisted.

She was out of bed now and eager to help find whatever it was, but Judy assured her there was nothing she could do.

"I saved a clue," she admitted, "but we can get along without it. Blackberry probably will provide a better one. When we find him we're sure to find whoever's playing ghost. I didn't tell you last night because you were crying, but I heard a cough behind the wall. Ghosts don't cough."

"But when we saw the—organist, he looked like Uncle David," Holly faltered.

"Maybe your uncle had a twin brother who looks exactly like him. If he had, then the brother could be working some trick in order to get hold of the property. Maybe he's a crook, and the family disowned him and never told anybody anything about him."

This seemed to Holly the most reasonable deduction Judy had yet come up with. But later on, when Judy questioned the relatives, they were positive that there was no twin.

"I certainly would have known of it. I was right in the house with my mother when David was born. I'm ten years older than he is, though I don't look it," Aunt Flo pointed out. "I'm sixty-eight."

"Just the age Grandma was when she died," thought Judy.

Somehow, Aunt Florence reminded her of her grandmother. Perhaps it was only because she was the oldest of the assembled relatives. Judy found herself feeling a little sorry for her. She probably had wanted to bring up Holly's sister Ruth chiefly because Diana had been such a disappointment to her. It had been wrong to separate the sisters, though.

As Judy thought it over she became so curious that she had to ask more questions. Aunt Flo's eyes narrowed.

"Doris, you've certainly forgotten plenty," she said. "You've forgotten how rebellious your little sister was, among other things. Why, we had to drag Holly away from her uncle, and only Cleo had the will to do it. I had enough on my hands with Diana always complaining."

"I didn't, Mamma," Diana protested childishly. "You just hovered over me until you made me ill."

"Someone had to look out for you," her mother snapped. "Look at the way you acted about that cat last night. There it was, sleeping on the bed as innocent as you please, and you let out such a shriek anybody would have thought it was a rattlesnake. By the way, where is the cat now? I haven't seen it around this morning."

"Have you seen it before?" Judy asked cautiously.

"Certainly. I think David used to feed it. Cleo tells me it's a stray, but a healthier-looking stray I never saw. It's surprisingly fond of you, too, I noticed."

"Of me?" asked Judy in pretended surprise.

"Certainly of you! Don't look so innocent. You and that cat know something you aren't telling. . . ."

"Maybe we do," Judy told Holly a few minutes later when she found her alone in the kitchen. "I just realized why Aunt Florence reminds me of my grandmother. She's wearing a purple dress the same shade as Grandma's, this morning. If only I could be sure—"

"There isn't time to be sure of anything now. We'll have to work fast," Holly interrupted. "Do you know why Aunt Florence is all dressed up? They expect Cousin Arlene to arrive at the airport this morning, and they're driving out to meet her. Doris may be with her for all I know. Anyway, she'll know you're not Doris."

"Cousin Cleo knows it already," Judy began.

"Yes, but she understands that you're trying to help me, but Cousin Arlene won't understand anything, and if I remember her, she won't give you a chance to explain. She'll think you're after the property, just like the rest of them. I'd leave here today, and let them fight it out among themselves if—"

"If what?" asked Judy as Holly looked off into space.

"If I didn't have a feeling that Uncle David would want us to solve the mystery back of this whole thing," Holly returned. "Come on, Judy, let's go back up to the music room and investigate some more. We may not have another chance!"

"Your relatives won't give us this chance if they find out what we're up to," Judy whispered as she and Holly stole upstairs and entered the music room, locking the door behind them.

"Holly! Doris!" they heard Aunt Flo calling impatiently. "Where are those girls?"

The car was waiting outside. Cousin Fred was ready to drive to the airport to meet the California cousin, Arlene Knight. Aunt Flo called again.

"They don't answer. We'll simply have to go without them," Judy heard Cousin Cleo say.

She and Holly were watching through the shutters. With the door safely locked, they knew their hiding place would not be discovered if they kept perfectly quiet until the relatives left. As Holly pointed out, this might be their last chance to find out anything.

Now, however, as they watched, a startling thing happened. Just as the car started, a black cat darted across the road in front of it. Judy held her breath and then let it out in a long, relieved gasp when she saw that the cat had not been hit.

"Blackberry!" she whispered. "Thank goodness, he's all right! I'd better go down and let him in."

"Yes, do. He may help us locate that secret door," Holly added.

"He isn't coming to the door," Judy observed. "He's going off toward Waldo Abson's barn. That's strange! Now somebody is letting him in. Your aunt Flo said your uncle used to feed him, but it must have been Waldo Abson. I wish Blackberry would pick people I like for his friends. You know, Holly, they say you never own a cat. You may own a dog. But a cat owns you."

"That's right," agreed Holly. "Cats are too independent."

"They crave freedom, like people," Judy said fondly. "I've always let Blackberry roam wherever he pleased. Usually he headed for the woods the minute I let him out. He wouldn't eat, either."

Holly laughed.

"No wonder, with your neighbors all feeding him!"

"I could tell that Waldo Abson a thing or two about cats!" Judy declared. "If he wants one, there are plenty of kittens being given away. Why doesn't he get his own?"

"I know why Uncle David didn't. His dog died about a year ago and he meant to get another. I wish he had. I like dogs," Holly said.

Judy was immediately on the defensive.

"Better than cats?"

Again Holly laughed.

"Not better than Blackberry. He's half human. Did you see the expression on Clyde's face when Blackberry streaked across in front of the car? Well, I'm glad they're gone. Now we can work undisturbed."

"Work, did you say? This is fun," declared Judy. "I brought my magnifying glass, and I intend to go over every inch of wall space. If those panels don't move, then something else is sure to. Do you want to try the organ now?"

Holly looked at it. Then she shivered.

"I—you—maybe you'd better," she stammered.

"Very well."

Putting aside her magnifying glass, Judy seated herself on the round organ stool and placed her feet on the pedals. Pumping hard, she began playing the few simple tunes she knew, stopping every now and them to push in or pull out another organ stop.

Nothing unusual happened. Judy noticed changes in tone and volume as she pulled out certain stops or pushed in others. But nothing else. One stop caused the music to become so loud that it left the room ringing with echoes.

Judy caught herself shivering this time.

"Let's leave the organ alone and try something else," Holly suggested. "I don't believe it's the organ anyway. It looks just the way it used to when Uncle David had it downstairs, and it surely didn't open any secret panel then."

"You remember the house well, don't you?" Judy asked. "Do you remember this room?"

Holly thought about it for a minute.

"I don't seem to. Anyway, I don't remember it the way it is now with the panels and the leafy wallpaper. It seems to me it used to be just an ordinary bedroom."

"Was it any larger than it is now?"

"Maybe. I don't remember."

"But the panels were put in recently?"

"Oh, yes!" Holly was sure. "They used to be in the dining room downstairs before it was redecorated.

The dining room did seem larger, but then I was smaller when I used to visit Uncle David. All the rooms seemed larger as I remember them. That molding on top used to be a plate rack when it was in the dining room. See how wide it is!"

"I do see. It's solid, though. I felt all along it last night and there isn't a break in it, but the panels below it are like doors all the way around the room. One of them must open. If only we could find out how—"

Judy stopped to listen.

"What's that?" asked Holly. "I thought I heard a cry."

"You did. It's Blackberry!" declared Judy. "He's behind this wall! He got in some way, and now he hears our voices and expects us to let him out."

"How can we?" asked Holly.

"We'll find a way." Judy was determined. One panel seemed loose. She pushed it in first one direction and then the other but it refused to slide either way.

"Maybe it lifts up and you crawl under," Holly suggested.

"How can it with the plate rack on top to stop it? I'll climb up and see, though."

Pulling over the organ stool, Judy climbed up to where she could look down on top of the plate rack and examine it through her magnifying glass.

"I've made a discovery!" she announced presently. "Blackberry must have leaped from the organ to the top of this panel. Here are his paw marks all along the plate rack. Do you think he could have pressed some secret button?"

Holly leaned wearily against the paneled wall.

"I'm sure I don't know how a cat could—"

She broke off suddenly as Judy slid her fingers along the wide strip of molding until she touched a small knob.

"This must be it. Holly!" she screamed as the whole wall seemed to give way and she saw the younger girl disappear through the dark opening behind it.

CHAPTER XXII

Trapped

"HOLLY, where are you?" Judy called anxiously.

Forgetting the knob under her fingers, Judy jumped down from the stool to see what had happened. But before she could discover how Holly had disappeared the panel slipped back in place and everything was just as it had been before.

"Holly! Holly! Are you all right? What happened to you?" called Judy as she pushed and pounded against the panel.

At first there was no answer. Then Blackberry's mournful *me-aurr!* sounded once more from behind the wall, and a hollow voice called:

"Watch yourself, Judy! Push the panel gently or you'll take a tumble the way I did."

"Are you hurt, Holly?"

"I'm all in one piece, though I did fall about eight feet," Holly admitted. "I felt like Alice in Wonderland tumbling down the rabbit hole. I thought I'd never stop. Luckily, there's hay at the bottom."

"Hay?"

"It feels like it and smells like it. There isn't any light down here so I can't be sure. Where's your flashlight?"

"I have it."

"Okay! There aren't any stairs, but there's a ladder. Blackberry's at the top of it. Just follow him and you'll be all right. Are you ready?"

"Ready for anything," Judy called back eagerly.

It took her but a moment to locate the knob she had touched before. This time she did not stand on the stool but reached up and pushed the knob with one hand while she pressed gently against the panel below it with the other. It swung back instantly to her touch revealing the dark opening down which Holly had tumbled.

A weird experience awaited Judy. At first she could see nothing at all except Blackberry's green eyes gleaming in the darkness. Then she turned on her flashlight and it showed her the ladder on which the cat was balancing himself. Cautiously she began to descend it, expecting him to follow.

"Come on, Blackberry!" she called. "You're supposed to show me the way."

But Blackberry, being an independent cat, had

other ideas. Quickly he leaped from the ladder into the room beyond it, and he was not a minute too soon. Before Judy could recover from her surprise at his strange behavior, the panel slipped back in place.

"That does it!" she exclaimed in exasperation. "Now we can't follow Blackberry. He's locked himself in the music room and there doesn't seem to be any way of opening the panel from this side."

"Never mind it now! There must be an opening at the other end," Holly called from below. "Come on down, Judy! I'm eager to explore. It's pitch dark down here, but I think there's a tunnel—"

"There is!" exclaimed Judy as her flashlight showed her a narrow passageway.

"Let's follow it! This is exciting. I feel like someone in a fairy tale," declared Holly. "What a story I can write when this adventure is over! Maybe little gnomes or elves live down here and dig for diamonds or something."

"Somebody has certainly been digging," agreed Judy, "but I doubt if it was little gnomes or elves. This really is a tunnel, and a long one. The sides are solid earth, but whoever dug it was smart enough to lay beams along the top to keep it from caving in. Hm! I'm begining to feel my direction, but I don't see any light at the other end."

"There must be an opening. Blackberry got in," Holly insisted.

"That cat has ways of getting in all sorts of places.

He got in Aunt Florence's room, didn't he?" asked
Judy.

Holly sighed. "We still haven't explained that one."

"There's plenty we haven't explained. But it won't
be long now," prophesied Judy. "I think we're coming to the end of this tunnel. Look, Holly! There's
another ladder!"

"So there is!" Holly exclaimed. "But where does it
go? There isn't any opening at the top."

"There must be," protested Judy, directing the
beam of her flashlight upward.

What she saw made her wonder how far she and
Holly had traveled underground. It had seemed only
a short distance, but now they were underneath another building. Judy was sure of it. She recognized
the beams overhead as part of the structure. Undoubtedly the second ladder led to still another secret entrance.

"It looks like a trap door," Judy observed when she
had climbed far enough up the ladder to examine the
boards overhead. "But how does it open?"

"Press against it!" Holly suggested.

"I am pressing, but it doesn't give an inch." Judy
pressed harder. "Oh dear!" she complained. "It must
be locked."

"Locked?" Holly's voice was panicky.

"I'm afraid so," Judy admitted. "There's no way
out at the other end and this trap door is certainly being held by something." She examined it with her

flashlight, then with her magnifying glass. "It's bolted," she announced. "There are hinges on one side of the door and a bolt on the other."

"Can't we—unscrew the hinges?"

Judy shook her head.

"The screws are on the other side."

"Then we're trapped in here! Somebody will have to let us out!" And, before Judy could warn her, Holly shouted, "Help! Help!" at the top of her voice.

Judy waited a moment until the echoes in the tunnel had faded into silence. Then she whispered, "Did you have to do that? It's spooky enough in here—"

Her sentence ended with a shiver as something scraped and rattled. It sounded right over Judy's head. Then she heard footsteps.

"Hel-lp!"

This time Holly's prolonged call brought no response whatsoever. Again Judy pressed against the overhead door. To her surprise, it opened easily.

"Well, what do you know?" she exclaimed as she poked her head through the opening. "Here we are, and you'd never guess where. In a barn! It must be Waldo Abson's barn. But who unbolted the door? There doesn't seem to be anybody here."

"There must be," Holly insisted.

She scrambled up the ladder and rushed to the outside door, shaking it angrily.

"We're still trapped!" she exclaimed. "He slipped

out, whoever he was, and locked us in here. What a mean trick! Now what are we going to do?"

"First we'll explore. We may find something important," declared Judy. "As for being trapped, I'm not worrying much about that. Eventually someone has to come in here to feed that calf over there in the pen. Isn't it cute, Holly? It looks like a brand-new one."

The two girls petted the baby calf's silky nose. Its pen was to the left of a row of stanchions for cows. Holly glanced at them hopefully. Then she remembered that it was still morning and a long wait until the cows would be let into the barn at milking time.

A mournful *moo!* sounded outside.

"There's the calf's mother," Judy observed. "When they let her in we'll find out what Waldo Abson is up to, if not before. I've suspected all along that he had a hand in this house haunting. He must have disguised himself as your uncle—"

"He isn't disguised now. There he is on his tractor. See!"

And Holly pointed out Judy's neighbor, who was working in a distant field. She had turned over an empty bushel basket and climbed up on it to peer out a high window. Judy looked, too.

"He looks innocent enough, doesn't he?" she asked. "I don't see how he got over there so quickly—that is, if it was he who unbolted that trap door. Maybe it was his wife who did. But no! There she is hanging out her washing. Neither of them acts as if they'd heard you calling for help, and I don't believe they did."

"Who did then?" asked Holly with a shiver.

"That's just what I'm wondering," declared Judy. "Certainly that newborn calf didn't, and it's the only living thing in here unless—"

"That's it!" Holly exclaimed as Judy paused to glance upward. "The hayloft! There's another ladder for us to climb!"

The two girls lost no time in ascending the ladder.

At the top Judy paused to look around. Then she called back to Holly, who was just behind her.

"It isn't a hayloft! Holly, look! You'll never believe it until you see it with your own eyes, but it's a regular apartment!"

"An apartment?" questioned Holly.

Judy, at the top of the ladder, was blocking her view.

"It looks like one. Anyway, there's a sleeping room. Someone's been hiding here, Holly!"

"Maybe it is a criminal! If he comes back and finds us here—oh, Judy! We've got to get out of here. There's a big window over there. Maybe it wouldn't be too high for us to jump!"

The two girls had taken a few steps into the loft. Judy caught hold of Holly's sweater sleeve.

"Wait!" she advised her. "Before we do anything foolish, let's have a look around."

CHAPTER XXIII

Discovered

At judy's suggestion, Holly soon calmed down and joined her in an investigation of the place. Instead of a hayloft, they discovered a room all fitted out with a cot and an old-fashioned washstand complete with bowl and pitcher.

"Someone has washed here this morning," Judy observed when she found the washcloth hanging on the rack of the washstand still a little damp.

The cot bed was made after a fashion. It looked as if a man had made it. A woman would have covered the pillow with the spread. Holly stood for a moment admiring it.

"What a pretty spread! It seems to me I've seen it before. Maybe it was Uncle David's, and this criminal stole it," she said.

"What criminal?" asked Judy absently.

She was busy exploring. Beyond the first room, separated by a half-partition, she discovered still another room, in which stood a bureau, a table and two chairs. On the table stood a plate and an empty cup. Both were unwashed.

"Don't touch them!" warned Judy as Holly came in and approached the table. "You may be right about a criminal hiding here. We don't want to spoil any fingerprints in case we have to call the police."

"The police!"

Judy had to laugh at Holly's horrified exclamation.

"You aren't afraid of policemen, are you?" she asked, still laughing. "It's their job to catch criminals."

"Of course. I didn't mean to sound like a little girl," confessed Holly. "It does look as if somebody's been hiding here and going in and out of my uncle's house whenever he pleased, doesn't it?"

"It surely does," agreed Judy. "What I can't understand is the tunnel. It took time to dig it—a lot of time. Your uncle would have known—"

"Maybe he did know," Holly interrupted.

Judy shook her head. She was really puzzled.

"This is an elaborate plan to trick somebody," she said at last. "There must be a disguise hidden up here somewhere, perhaps in this old bureau."

"Let's look," Holly suggested, pulling open the top drawer.

"What is it?" asked Judy as Holly gave a gasp of surprise.

"His music!" Holly let out a long breath. "It's here! Uncle David's music is here. Look, Judy! Here's the song, 'Wanting Too Much,' * just the way he wrote it."

Judy did look. In fact, she stared. The whole drawer was filled with musical compositions written in pencil on lined music paper. The words to each song were carefully printed. Some had been inked in, but most were in pencil.

"Here's one I remember," she said, taking a sheet from the pile. "Your uncle sang it to me when I was thirteen. I think I remember the tune:

> " *'She's only thirteen,*
> *But she's proud as a queen.*
> *She's right out amongst them,*
> *This maid of thirteen.' " **

"I remember it," Holly nodded, when Judy had finished singing the chorus. "He wrote it for Doris. She was proud, too, and so pretty. How I would love to see her," she added wistfully.

"Maybe you will—and soon. I hear a car coming along the road." Judy ran to the window. "It is!" she exclaimed. "Your relatives have come back, and there's a red-haired girl with them. There's a stout, blonde woman, too."

* *By Victor L. Beebe*

"That's Cousin Arlene. Oh, I'm so glad Doris came with her. But Judy, what will you do?"

Judy laughed.

"I'll go home where I belong. Peter may be back by now."

"First, we have to get out of here," Holly reminded her.

"And before we do that," Judy added, searching through the remaining drawers in the dresser, "we have to find an answer to a question that just popped into my mind. There isn't any disguise. You can see that for yourself."

Two of the drawers contained music, much of it old sheet music that looked valuable, at least to a collector, and the rest handwritten. In the other three drawers were the usual things anyone might expect to find in a dresser—socks, shirts, ties, underwear, handkerchiefs all neatly laundered, but nothing of special significance.

"This is strange. I'm beginning to wonder—"

But what Holly was beginning to wonder Judy was not to hear. At that moment the barn door opened and a voice shouted up from the floor below.

"Hey! What's going on up there? I don't allow tramps in my barn."

"It's Waldo Abson," Holly whispered.

"Good!" exclaimed Judy. "He's just the man I wanted to see." Aloud she called, "You certainly allowed somebody up here, Mr. Abson. We've discovered sleeping quarters—"

"Sleeping quarters? You don't say!"

Waldo Abson's head appeared above the open trap for the ladder.

"Well! Well!" he drawled. "If that don't beat all! Sleeping quarters in my old hayloft. If that don't beat all! Now who would have suspected a thing like that?"

"Didn't you know about it?" demanded Judy, annoyed that he should treat the matter as a joke. "I don't suppose you know about the tunnel, either, or the secret entrance to the Potter house."

"Secret entrance? Sounds like a piece of fiction," he commented. "No wonder folks thought the house was haunted!"

Judy's eyes narrowed.

"I have a pretty good idea who was haunting it, Mr. Abson. If you were a little taller and not quite so heavy-set—"

"Me? Have I any reason for haunting the Potter house?"

"You seem to have a reason for wanting it haunted. I don't know who else it could be, unless—"

"See here," he interrupted, "before you start accusing an innocent neighbor, I suggest you investigate that impostor who calls himself Clyde Potter."

"Impostor or not, it wasn't Clyde who was playing

the organ," Judy retorted. "It scared him half **to** death."

"Scared him, eh?"

Waldo Abson chuckled.

"I reckon that's what David Potter's ghost was aiming to do. David always said he'd come back and haunt his relatives if they started squabbling over his property, and by gum, he's kept his word."

Judy shook her head. That sort of talk was getting them nowhere.

"Mr. Abson," she said seriously, "if you know something about this ghost business, won't you please help us? We're at our wits' end, Holly and I. We don't believe in ghosts, and you don't either!"

"Seeing is believing," he chuckled.

"Not always. Someone could have disguised himself as David Potter."

"You think so? A pretty good disguise, I would say. David Potter was my best friend. I'd know him anywhere."

"Did you see him?" Judy asked point-blank.

Her neighbor blinked. "See him? How could I see him?"

"That's just what I was wondering," Judy said.

Holly looked bewildered. It was obvious that they would get no help from Waldo Abson, although he had no objections to their ghost chasing, as he called it. He even added a little apology on behalf of the ghost.

"I don't believe he aimed to lock you girls in," Waldo Abson drawled, as he opened the barn door. "I usually leave this open. Far as I'm concerned, you can come and go as you please. You and the ghost and his black cat—"

"His black cat!" exclaimed Judy. "*His* black cat!"

"But the cat is yours, Judy," Holly protested, as the girls hurried out, "if he meant Blackberry—"

"He does mean Blackberry! I'm sure of it!" exclaimed Judy. "That cat had a clue for me all the time if I'd only had the sense to follow it. Come on, Holly! There isn't any time to lose."

"Where are we going?" asked Holly as Judy pulled her along.

"Back to your uncle's house. You want to see your sister, don't you?"

"Of course I do. I can't wait to see her. But what'll we tell her?"

"Plenty," declared Judy.

They had reached the Potter house. Doris was nowhere in sight. At the door they were met by the newcomer, Arlene Knight. Her stout figure blocked the doorway. She glared at Judy.

"So you're the girl who calls herself Doris Potter, are you?" she asked sarcastically. "Why, there isn't even a resemblance except for the red hair. The real Doris Potter is here, and you—"

"I know," Judy admitted, "and I confess I'm a fake. Holly's real, though—"

"I doubt it."

The hostile gaze of the woman at the door shifted to Holly. Her face was smudged and her hands were black. So were Judy's. After all, they had spent the last two hours crawling through a tunnel and exploring a barn. What could anyone expect?

"If you'll let us come in and wash—" Holly began, but Arlene would not let her finish.

"Neither of you put a foot inside this door! This girl admits she's a fake, and you certainly aren't Holly—"

"Me? Not Holly?"

Holly looked at Judy as if the idea fascinated her. "Maybe I'm a changeling. Maybe an old witch left me."

Cousin Arlene was not amused.

"Well, whoever you are, you'll have to find some other place to stay."

Holly bristled.

"What about Doris? I haven't seen her for seven years and I'm not going to be cheated out of the chance now."

"Cheated!" Arlene sniffed. "You're the one who's doing the cheating."

"Anyway, I want my clothes!"

"I'll set your suitcase outside. Doris and I will need the room—"

"Oh, thanks!" Holly was furious. "That's so good

of you, Arlene," she said sarcastically. "I suppose I
can live in someone's barn. Odd that I never thought
of it."

She stopped speaking as Arlene slammed the door.

Ten minutes later it opened again, and two suitcases slid outside. The girls had a glimpse of Clyde
peering at them through the window, but still no
sign of Doris.

"They haven't told Doris I'm here. They're keeping
me away from her deliberately," Holly began.

"We've discovered something, and they know it.
Anyway, Clyde does, and he's afraid the others will
find out. Blackberry's in there, too, and Clyde hates
him with good reason. We've got to get my cat out
of there, and we're going to need help. Let's hurry
back to my house and telephone."

CHAPTER XXIV

Accused

"HORACE!" exclaimed Judy.

The two girls had hurried along the path through
the woods to find Judy's brother sitting morosely on
her front porch.

"Well, it's about time you came home. If this is a
haunted house, the ghost is awfully quiet—"

"Wrong house. My mistake," Judy interrupted.

She was out of breath from hurrying. Horace took
the suitcases and they all went inside.

"Holly is going to stay with us. They won't let her
back in her uncle's house. Horace, you've got to help
us," Judy implored. "Holly's sister is here and they
won't even let them see each other."

"The sister who looks like you?" Horace questioned.

"She doesn't really. Just her hair." Judy was washing her hands and face as she talked. "Now I look a little more like myself, anyway," she announced as Holly took her turn at the sink. "As I said before, you've got to help us, Horace. We've been locked out of the house and Blackberry's locked in."

"How did that happen?" asked Horace.

"How did it all happen!" exclaimed Judy. "It's fantastic, no matter how you figure it out. There's a secret panel, and a tunnel, and Holly thinks a criminal may be hiding in Waldo Abson's barn. Certainly, someone is! Mr. Abson knows it, too, but he just stands and chuckles and won't admit a thing. The barn door's open, though. We can get back into the Potter house through the tunnel—"

"Wait a minute," Horace stopped her. "First I'd like to know something about these transparent people you were telling me about. I followed your instructions to the letter and exactly at the right time, too, but I didn't see a thing, so I came back this morning. I've been here since six o'clock and I might as well tell you I'm sick of hanging around when nothing happens—and on the newspaper's time! I've got to bring in some sort of a story."

"You will. It's going to be a honey, too," Judy prophesied. "You can spread it all over the front page, and maybe even photograph the transparent people. But first let's rescue Blackberry. He's locked in the music room and Clyde Potter may kill him if he gets in there ahead of us. Come on, Horace, let's hurry!"

"What if Peter comes home? You're expecting him, aren't you?"

"Any time now, but we can't wait."

On a large piece of paper Judy scrawled: *Peter! Look for us at the Potter house. We may be in trouble. Love, Judy.* She propped it up on the table right where Peter would see it the minute he came in. Then she and Holly and Horace left, not taking the short-cut through the woods. Instead, they cut straight through the pasture and went directly to Waldo Abson's barn.

"Good!" exclaimed Judy, breathless from running.

He had left the door open as he had promised he would. After a brief inspection of the place, Horace decided to try the tunnel.

"If you hear a scream," he said jokingly, "you'll know I've met the ghost."

"Don't make a sound if you meet him. No matter how startled you are, just keep your head and think of that story you wanted." Judy was deadly serious.

As Horace disappeared through the trap door she had real fears for his safety. And when, half an hour later, he still had not returned, she decided to follow him.

"You stay here in the barn," she told Holly. "I may find myself trapped, too. If I'm not back in five minutes, go for the police."

"Me?" asked Holly. "Go for the police? How?"

"Use my telephone. I'll give you the key to my house and to the locked room in case you need it—"

She broke off quickly as the trap door banged. It was a minute before she dared breathe. Then Horace's head appeared through the opening.

"Nice concert!" he commented as the two girls stared at him. "Your ghost plays the organ exceedingly well. I've just been listening. I suspect your relatives are doing a little listening themselves, Holly. I could hear shouts and screams and an occasional chuckle. It was quite a performance."

"But you didn't get in?"

"No. I knocked, but the ghost didn't want company. Blackberry is with him. His yowls at the end of each strain of music were quite effective. The house was in an uproar. I wasn't the only one knocking. I heard a voice threatening to break the door down—"

"Cousin Clyde, I'll bet." Holly was excited.

"This time they will let me in," declared Judy. "I'll tell them that I have the key!"

Horace approved of this idea, but Holly hung back.

"It's dangerous," she protested. "You don't know what you'll be walking into."

She was right, of course, but Judy had walked into danger before, and was not afraid.

"Your sister is there. She won't let anyone hurt you—"

"I'll see that no one escapes through the tunnel," Horace promised, placing a milk stool over the trap door and seating himself upon it.

"You may be in more danger than we are," Judy warned him as she and Holly, convinced that it was the only thing to do, left for the house.

They were admitted, rather ungraciously, by Aunt Florence after Judy had shouted up to her that she had the key.

Everybody was on the second floor, listening outside the door of the music room. Doris was there and recognized Holly immediately.

"My poor little sister!" she exclaimed, clasping her in her arms and almost smothering her with kisses. "Nobody told me you were here. And is this—but of course it is! You're Judy Bolton, aren't you? I remember you in pigtails, but I've seen your picture in the paper and read of your detective work—"

Judy put her finger to her lip. But she was too late. Clyde had heard. His eyes became slits in his face—slits filled with hatred.

"So you're a detective, are you?" he asked. "I knew there couldn't be two Doris Potters. One of you had to be a phony, but I suspected her."

He jerked his thumb toward Doris, who looked at Judy apologetically, but there was nothing much she could do now that she had given her away.

"I'm a phony all right," agreed Judy, "and I suspect

you are, too. If I'm right about the musician in there you're going to have something to explain, Clyde Potter, and very soon."

Saying this, Judy started toward the door of the music room. But Clyde was ahead of her.

"Keep away!" he warned her, blocking her path. "Whoever is in there is mad. There's no telling what harm he may do if you let him loose."

"Mad, is he? I doubt it," said Judy. "I believe we're all in full possession of our senses, and right now the thing to do is to open this door—with the key!"

The music had stopped. Everything seemed to stop for a moment. Then, with the swiftness of a cat, Clyde sprang toward Judy and seized her hand.

"Give me that key," he gritted in her ear. "Nobody goes in that room ahead of me. I'm the closest relative."

"Are you?" asked Judy skeptically.

Clyde stared at her. So did all the others.

"I'm his son. You saw the birth certificate."

"I've seen birth certificates that weren't genuine before. And photographs! You were almost too convincing, Clyde Potter—if that is your name. No you don't!" cried Judy, as he began twisting her wrist.

"See here, what are you afraid of? I'm beginning to suspect you myself," declared Cousin Fred, swinging Clyde around. "If anyone goes in that room first, I intend to—"

"You're too late, Cousin Fred," Holly interrupted. "Judy and I have already been in. There's a secret exit and a tunnel leading to Waldo Abson's barn, but it's being watched at the other end. The—the ghost can't escape."

"We've both seen him," Judy added.

Clyde's face blanched.

"Then you know—"

"Know what?" Judy interrupted, making a wild guess. "That you're not his son?"

His face told her that she had guessed correctly. Blackberry must have sensed his mistress' triumph, for a long-drawn-out yowl came from the other side of the locked door.

"I'll kill that cat if I get my hands on him," Clyde declared viciously.

"I wouldn't do that if I were you," a voice from the doorway advised quietly.

It was Peter! Judy's heart did a rapid somersault, but she gave no sign that she recognized him. Quickly unlocking the door, she swung it wide.

"Well, what do you know? It's empty!" Cousin Fred exclaimed.

He was right. No one was in the room, no one at all except a frightened black cat who immediately leaped to the plate rack for safety. Blackberry landed squarely upon the button that opened the secret panel. It slipped open as if by magic. Behind it, to the utter amazement of everybody, stood David Potter—very much alive.

Doris was the first to recover from the shock of seeing him.

"Uncle David!" she cried as he stepped from the top of the ladder out into the room. Horace was just behind him, his face beaming with satisfaction when he saw that Peter was there. Judy was right. This would be a story that he could spread all over the front page of the newspaper. Only Holly refused to believe it.

"You aren't—you can't be—" she began. "Uncle David, if you're really you, how did you make yourself transparent? You—you looked like a g-ghost!"

"But he isn't. He's real!" cried Doris, throwing her arms about the startled old man. "Oh, I'm so glad!"

In that same instant everybody turned to stare at the man who had identified David Potter's body in the wreck—the man who called himself Clyde Potter.

"I—I must have made a mistake," the young man defended himself weakly.

"You've made plenty of mistakes, Durk Dugan. Big ones, too." Peter's voice was quiet. "But the biggest mistake of all was when you turned to crime for an easy living. It never works."

"You can't prove a thing. I made a mistake, that's all," the man muttered.

"He certainly had me fooled for a while. Is his

name really Durk Dugan, Peter?" Judy asked.

"We don't know for sure yet. It may be only one of his aliases," Peter explained, "but Durk Dugan is the name of a confidence man wanted for a list of crimes as long as your arm. Your description of Clyde Potter fitted a composite picture we had made up of him. His business is being the long-lost relative who needs money to attend a funeral or a wedding or a family reunion."

"Not a very pleasant business," one of the relatives commented. Judy didn't notice which one it was. She was watching Holly approach her uncle a little timidly. She seemed afraid to go too near him.

"I'm real," David Potter told her gently. "Come here and touch me, Holly, my little Christmas girl. Then you'll believe it. I didn't mean to frighten *you*, child. I didn't figure you'd be here."

"But you were—transparent. I could see right through you—"

"That is something for you to explain, Uncle David," put in Cousin Cleo. "Judy told us the same thing."

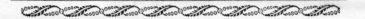

CHAPTER XXV

The Transparent People

DAVID POTTER seemed to be as bewildered by this as all the others.

"Transparent?" he questioned. "Where did you girls see this—this apparition?"

"In Judy's garden."

"Impossible!" he exclaimed. "I wasn't there. I took great pains to keep out of sight for fear I would frighten someone—"

"And so you took the path through the woods, didn't you?" asked Judy.

He admitted it.

"Once or twice I did. I saw Holly there once. Oh, I got around. I managed to let you girls out of the barn without being caught. I listened outside your house when you and Holly were talking, too. I didn't hear a good word from either of you. It seemed that my will was all you cared about—"

"It wasn't, Uncle David! I cared about you!" cried Holly. "I was just putting on an act to keep my heart from breaking. I'd rather have you alive and loving me than all the property in the world!"

"I knew that later, when I heard you crying. Well, you've got me."

He chuckled as Holly rushed into his arms. Aunt Florence bristled.

"If this was a joke," she said, "it wasn't a very funny one. Explain yourself, David! You may be my own brother, but this time you've carried your teasing a little too far."

"You're right, Flo," he confessed, looking a little sheepish. "It backfired on me. I didn't mean to mix Holly up in it, although I may as well admit that I did plan to have this young reporter on the scene when the story broke."

"Me?" asked Horace, a little bewildered himself. "So that explains that weird communication from Florida?"

"Yep! I hoped you'd find out what this young scoundrel who calls himself my son was up to—with the help of your sister, of course, and her FBI husband—"

"FBI!" Clyde's face went white. Without another

word, he made a dash for the stairs. Peter did not attempt to stop him, but let him walk right into the arms
of one of the policemen he had brought with him.

Suddenly the house seemed filled with policemen.
"Clyde Potter" was very quickly handcuffed and
held by two of them, as everybody crowded into the
music room to hear the rest of David Potter's strange
story.

"You have a thing or two to explain, yourself," one
of the officers said roughly to the prisoner.

"Me? What's the use?" He glared at Peter and
added, "I might have known that guy was a Fed. He's
snooped out everything."

"My wife is the one who deserves the credit for
what we have learned," Peter said honestly.

"I just wanted to help Holly," Judy explained.
"Yes, and you too, Mr. Potter. Your will was burned,
and your son—I mean, this man—stole even the one
legible scrap I found in the fireplace—"

"My will!" David Potter exclaimed. "But I never
made one! If you found a will, it must have been
forged. Flo, you didn't—"

"I had to, David. I couldn't let him get away with
everything. I knew he wasn't your son, but I had no
proof, and I do need money for Diana—"

"Let her work for it!" snapped David Potter. "Do
her good. Work never hurt anybody yet."

"Forgery is a serious offense," Peter said gravely.

"I know it. Oh, what will they do to me?"

Aunt Florence collapsed into a chair and began to sob brokenly. Judy actually felt sorry for her. Every one of the relatives looked embarrassed, even the new-comer, Arlene Knight. It was she who urged her uncle to go on with his story.

"It was your so-called son who burned the forged will, I suppose? Can't we just forget it?" she asked.

"I'm willing, if it's okay with Peter Dobbs here, but neither Flo nor her precious Diana will be mentioned when I do make a will—"

His sister looked at him gratefully.

"Anything, David, if you will only forgive us."

"I'll consider it," the old man replied, and Judy had the feeling he was enjoying himself, "but I want no mercy shown to the crook who burned the forged will. And isn't falsely identifying a body a criminal offense?"

Peter assured him that it was.

"What did happen in Florida, Mr. Potter?" Judy asked curiously. "You suspected this man wasn't your real son when you went down there to check up on him, didn't you?"

"I was sure of it," David Potter declared, "but I had to have proof. My own son was ill from the day of his birth. He couldn't have lived to grow up."

A gasp went around the room. So that was it!

"But the birth certificate! The pictures! How do you explain them?" asked Cousin Cleo.

"Suppose we let Dugan explain them himself," Peter suggested in a tone that left the criminal very little choice.

Dugan shrugged. "I knew Clyde's half brother and got the dope from him," he said. "He's the boy in most of the pictures. Potter's right. His own kid did die very young. But his wife married again, and her second son looked like the first one. We doped this thing out together, and it would have been a good racket if it hadn't been for that bad-luck cat—"

"Bad luck for criminals," Judy interrupted, picking Blackberry up to cuddle him in her arms. "This isn't the first time he's helped us, is it, Peter?"

"You're right, Judy," he returned, "and it probably won't be the last."

As the impostor was led away, Peter turned to David Potter.

"Now you can really relax," he said. "Why don't you make yourself comfortable in your own easy chair, and tell us the rest of your story? We'll listen."

"We sure will!" agreed Horace, his black notebook ready. "You were suspicious of this criminal when he first got in touch with you, claiming to be your son, weren't you?"

"Yes, but I was suspicious of the whole lot of them," David Potter declared. "They left me strictly alone when I was poor, but the minute it came out in the papers that gas had been discovered on my property, they were all anxious to come and live with me

—even my supposed son, whom I hadn't seen or heard from since he was a little baby. I thought I'd invite them for a family reunion and show them the error of their ways. Waldo and I rigged up the tunnel and the two trap doors with the idea of doing a little house haunting. We figured," the old man chuckled, "that by the time we got through with them they wouldn't be so anxious to make my home their home. It was just a joke at first."

"A pretty grim joke, I should say," Cousin Cleo remarked, but her uncle had not finished.

"Well, as I was saying," he continued, "all the relatives accepted except this fellow who claimed to be my son. He wired that he needed funds. So I decided to go down there and see what was what. Well, he pretty nearly convinced me with his smooth answers and all the family records and pictures. I was almost ready to believe a medical miracle had taken place and my son had lived after all."

Peter shook his head. "You aren't the first one he's fooled, Mr. Potter. He could have had a great career as an actor if he had turned his talents in the right direction."

"I believe you. He almost had me fooled all right," David Potter went on. "We were on our way back here when this hurricane struck. I was hurled through a broken window and into a swamp. I swam for a little way under all that mossy stuff that grows down there in Florida. Then I began to lose my strength, and the next thing I knew, I was in a little board cabin. A young colored boy had dragged me out of the swamp, and his kind old mother had 'brung me back to life,' as she put it. Funny part of it was, I felt fine, not a scratch on me. That is, I did feel fine until I got into the nearest town and saw the papers. There was *my* name—among the known dead. At first I was mad— mad as a hornet. 'Identified by his son,' it said. Then I got to thinking about that reunion and wondering what would have happened if I really had died. Well, sir, I made up my mind to find out."

"And in doing so helped trap a vicious criminal," Peter added.

"Oh, Uncle David, we're so proud of you!" exclaimed Doris. "Holly and I have wanted to see you and each other, but Cousin Arlene insisted it would only make trouble, and traveling is so expensive—"

"Well, you're here to stay now, if you can stand your old uncle's eccentricities."

"You aren't eccentric, Uncle David," Holly protested. "You're just like a detective in a story, and we *are* proud of you!"

"Hm! I can't say I'm very proud of myself," he admitted. "I misjudged you, for one thing. They say that eavesdroppers never hear any good of themselves. I should have remembered that, when I was snooping and listening—"

"Behind my house!" Judy interrupted excitedly as the last piece of the amazing puzzle she had been trying to solve fell into place. "No wonder Blackberry kept yowling to be fed! He knew you were there and you always fed him. What we saw was your *reflection* in the garden. It did look like a ghost, but now I think I've figured out exactly what happened."

"You have?" Horace was all interest. "But you saw Grandma's reflection, too, and she really is dead."

"Aunt Florence isn't. You don't mind if I keep on calling you Aunt Florence, do you?" Judy asked the older woman beside her.

"I'm surprised you want to own me for a relative," she returned humbly. "David doesn't. He can call me anything he pleases. I'm a greedy old woman who put money ahead of love, and I'm downright ashamed of myself. I wanted too much, just like your song said, David—"

"We all did," put in Cousin Cleo. "We're all to blame for what happened and for the way we've treated these poor girls. We'll have to make it up to Ruth, too."

"Poor Ruth," Diana murmured. "Mother and I didn't make her very happy."

"I'm afraid Holly hasn't been very happy with us either," Cousin Fred sighed. "We were the transparent people. But this clever little neighbor of yours saw right through us. We're truly sorry, Uncle David."

Holly was really puzzled now.

"You said it was a reflection, Judy. Is that all it was? How did you find out?"

"By using my head," returned Judy, "but I still have to see it again to make sure."

"You will," Horace prophesied, closing his notebook. He had his story now, and was eager to get back to the office with it.

Judy's demonstration took place a few days later. Afterwards everybody declared it was the strangest sight they had ever witnessed. All of Holly's relatives except Aunt Florence and Diana were there in Judy's living room watching. The Potter family reunion had turned out to be a real one, and the guests had overflowed into Judy's home. Among them was Holly's oldest sister, Ruth, with her husband and baby. Horace arrived at the house last of all, and Honey was with him. Although he had spread his haunted-house story all over the paper, he had yet to see the now famous "ghosts."

"I can't believe it, although Horace's story was convincing," Honey admitted.

Judy's eyes sparkled with fun as she turned to Peter.

"You go first," she told him. "I've never yet seen through you, but now I will. And take Blackberry, the black cat that's bad luck for criminals, bless him!"

Blackberry didn't care for the idea at all. He clung firmly to his place on David Potter's knee.

The old man chuckled. "Blackberry was with me

last evening in the music room," he said. "I opened the hall door to sneak a look-see, and he darted out. He must have gotten into Flo's room somehow, and gone to sleep. I heard Diana yelling her head off later," he added with another chuckle, "and I knew then where that cat must be!"

"That was the thing that convinced me there must be another, secret, entrance to the house," declared Judy. She laughed. "You never do own a cat, do you? But I don't mind sharing Blackberry with my favorite neighbors. I can see through him already. 'He loveth best who feedeth best.' " She laughed again as Horace grimaced. "Maybe I'm mixed up on my quotations, but my deductions are right. He wasn't catching his dinner in the woods as I thought. He's been getting free lunches at the Potter farm. Here, take him, Peter, before he betrays me completely."

And she placed the unwilling cat in Peter's arms.

"Now go out the back door and walk toward that shortcut through the woods. Watch, everybody!" she directed. "It's four o'clock and the sun is just right. In a minute you'll see Peter's 'ghost' in the garden."

Presently it appeared. Judy was not surprised, although the transparent reflection did startle Holly and the others a little. Afterwards, she and her sisters tried it, and then everybody took turns being "ghost."

At last it was clear to everyone. A person walking in the sunlight *back* of the house would cast a reflection in the window looking out on the garden, when that window was in shadow.

"We looked out the wrong window!" Holly exclaimed, understanding at last. "The reflection is cast from the opposite window, isn't it? The window behind us? I still can't understand why you thought you saw your grandmother, though, Judy."

"It was Aunt Florence," Judy explained. Aunt Florence was not present at the demonstration. She and her daughter had left that morning. "It was really the purple dress that startled me. It was reflected quite vividly, and Grandma did have one almost exactly like it."

Holly had to think about this for a moment.

"We'll probably never know just why Aunt Flo sneaked around back of your house," she began.

"She could have come from that path through the woods," Horace suggested.

"That's it!" Judy exclaimed. "It is a shortcut to the main road from your uncle's house on the other side of the hill."

"In that case," Holly declared, "we three girls will be using it quite often—with your permission, Judy."

To Judy's surprised question, David Potter explained that he had invited all three of his nieces to make their home with him.

"Ruth's husband will take the place of the son I lost, and the girls will be like daughters," he said.

Judy was delighted. "They'll be perfect neighbors," she told Peter.

Although she didn't know her "perfect neighbors" would soon involve her in another mystery, she was confident that something exciting was in store for her. As David Potter had said in his song:

> "The world is wide, the sky is blue,
> The future fair is waiting you."

Judy and Peter were young. They were in love. The future was very fair for them. And they were ready for anything it had to offer them.

Judy's friendship with the Potter family soon involves her in one of the most thrilling of all her adventures. It is not until she has learned the answers to three questions that Judy finally finds the solution of an old, old mystery, in

THE FORBIDDEN BOX.